FOURTEEN
pomegranate
SEEDS

KHAJA NIZAMUDDIN

BLUEROSE PUBLISHERS
India | U.K.

Copyright © Khaja Nizamuddin 2023

All rights reserved by author. No part of this publication may be reproduced, stored in a retrieval system or transmitted in any form or by any means, electronic, mechanical, photocopying, recording or otherwise, without the prior permission of the author. Although every precaution has been taken to verify the accuracy of the information contained herein, the publisher assumes no responsibility for any errors or omissions. No liability is assumed for damages that may result from the use of information contained within.

BlueRose Publishers takes no responsibility for any damages, losses, or liabilities that may arise from the use or misuse of the information, products, or services provided in this publication.

For permissions requests or inquiries regarding this publication, please contact:

BLUEROSE PUBLISHERS
www.BlueRoseONE.com
info@bluerosepublishers.com
+91 8882 898 898
+4407342408967

ISBN: 978-93-5704-122-5

Cover design: Muskan Sachdeva
Typesetting: Pooja Sharma

First Edition: November 2023

Dedication

I dedicate my book to my father, Mohammed Jalaaluddin, a teacher who couldn't see the impact of his love and training on me because of his untimely death.

To my mother, Syeda Tahera Bano, who infused manners and taught me the lessons of love, tolerance and honesty, passing through thick and thin.

Acknowledgement

I feel great to credit my guide, Professor G. Laxminarayana, Vice Chancellor Kuppam, University with transforming me from an English teacher to a translator. I am really grateful to him because, like an elder brother, he gave me shelter in Potti Sree Ramulu Telugu University and helped me join Ph.D. He made me scribble a few pages on Deccan literature, and it became a basis for me to take up the work of translation.

My acknowledgement to my wife, Mrs. Rafat Farzana, retired Vice Principal of Lal Bahadur College, Warangal, the driving force behind this work of translation.

I would like to express my indebtedness to my children,

Dr. Farhana Afreen Naaz, M.S., ENT MRCS, DOHNS, UK, for her encouragement. I thank my son-in-law Mirza Sajid Ali Baig, B. Tech, my son Dr. Khusro Nizam Zameer, MS ENT, and my daughter-in-law Dr. Lubna Noor MBBS.

My grandchildren, Mirza Aaqib Sajid Baig and Aleena Mariam Sajid, were the only ones who ever forced me to write books. Juveria, Zara Zameer, my granddaughter, as well as Faizan-e-Mujtaba Zameer, for occasionally distracting me to refresh my mind.

I am highly grateful to my teachers, Mohamed Abdul Lateef Shareef, my English teacher, for giving me the base.

It would be impolitic if I didn't express my abundant gratitude to the Blue Rose Publishing team that patiently brought me out of my shell and favourably exposed my writings to the outer world.

About The Writer

I was born on 9-7-1955. I schooled in a government Urdu medium school Urus Jagir Warangal Telangana India, which is a resting place of Saint Mashooq Rabbani RA. He is the 11th direct descendent of Qutbe Rabbani, Mahboobe Subhani, Ghouse Samdani Hazrat Abdul Qadir Jilani RA. From middle school to intermediate, I was at Islamia High School. I did my graduation from the prestigious University Arts College in Subedari and my postgraduate work at Kakatiya University in Warangal.

After post-graduation I joined Chandra Kanthaiah Memorial College, Warangal as a part-timer in January 1980. One year I worked in Mahboobia Panjetan Junior College, Warangal, and in 1981 I joined my mother institute, Islamia Arts and Science College, Warangal. I worked at the Dr. BR Ambedkar Study Center for Urdu-medium students. I also worked at the School of Distant Learning and Continuing Education at Kakatiya University, Warangal. While working as a lecturer, I worked as a programme officer of NSS unit. I did a special camp in Gurrekunta, Home for the Aged, and as Adult Education Program Officer, I opened adult education centers in three places. I opened Jana Shikshna Nilayam in Central Prison, Warangal, and organised Holi and Eid Milap programs. I arranged free coaching at the College for Edcet. and Icet., under the UGC.

I retired as a lecturer in 2013 and joined as English faculty at Shadan Institute of Engineering and Technology, peerancheru Hyderabad. I worked at

Shadan College of Pharmacy and taught "value-based education" and "gender sensitization" there. Simultaneously, I worked as an inspecting authority at the Maulana Azad Educational Foundation under the auspices of the Ministry of Minority Affairs. I worked in this position for four years and inspected about twelve NGO-run centers.

No wrong if I declare myself an autodidact. Yes, but Ibne Safi is the man who taught me Urdu, attitude, and behavior. I accept my students taught me language. I was guided by Prof S.K. Ram from the National Council of Educational Research and Training and Yadav Rajan from the State Council of Educational Research and Training and CFL. For my inclination towards translation and comparative studies, the credit goes to the kind-hearted Professor Vice Chancellor of Kuppam University, who guided me in the field of translation, Professor G Laxminarayan. He asked me to take up Deccan literature to translate. I translated about twenty-five poems by Quli Qutb Shah. Even today, from the United States of America, he continues to guide and encourage me. I started writing short stories from my graduation days but did not publish them. I have selected Deccan writers for my translation work. I planned to publish them in a chronological order. This is my first book and the second one is in process. I left no stone unturned to convey the message of writers to the non-Urdu readers.

Email:khajanizamuddin1818@gmail.com

Phone:9849306918

LinkedIn: khaja Nizamuddin

WhatsApp:9849306918

Foreword

Sabaq phir Padh sadaqat ka adalat ka, shujaat ka

Liya jayega tujh se kaam duniya ki imamat ka

Deccan is a Centre for learning right from the beginning. It has given birth to so many stalwarts in Urdu literature. Some writers were born here and spread worldwide as bellwethers bearing a torch of literature, and some writers were born in other parts of India and joined the Deccan Row of Urdu writers. I have selected quite a few from among them and arranged them in chronological order. The book's spine is too narrow to accommodate all the writers of Deccan, so I have decided to write in three volumes, and Insha Allah, if life permits, I will try to materialize my dream. Things went along smoothly after the writers sent their books personally and extended their maximum support. I needed to collect profiles of the writers and some stories from "Rekhta" and "Rekhta Nama." I hope I am everything a translation project could want. I tried my best to do justice with the stories and the profiles of the writers. I found my feet in the field of translation, and I hope it stands the test of time. Despite my attempt to present what the writer intends, most of the time the feeling of kissing a face from behind the veil, remains.

I was fond of reading and writing from the beginning. When we were in eighth grade, two seniors from our school, Dr Mubashir Ahmed and Dr Mahmood Ahmed, established a reading centre named "Nishane-Rah." They initiated to issue a pen magazine. It had a wonderful impact on me and made me inclined toward reading and writing.

As I grew, I became a lover of reading Ibne Safi's "Jasoosi Duniya." Rumani Duniya, the writings of Adil Rasheed. In magazines, I was fond of reading "Bisween Sadi," "Shama," "Ruby," and so on. Among the writers I read are Munshi Prem Chand, Sadat Hasan Manto, Krishna Chander, Quratul Ain Haider, and Fikar Tounsiwi. I watched the caricature of Zafar Nizami. I cannot come out of the impact of Prem Chand's Kafan. Krishan Chander's "Dil ki wadiyan so gayeen," "Rabar ki Aurat," and Manto's "Toba Tek Singh." "Thanda Gosht," "Kali Shalwar," and Quratul Ain Haider's "Chaye ke Baaghaat." Khaja Ahmed Abbas', novel, "Saath Hindustani," his short stories, "Diya Jale sari Raat," and "Sparrows," have great impact on my mind. After reading different stories, I used to discuss the themes with my intimate friend Khaja Habeeb Ahmed, the former DGM in HTD in Andhra Pradesh.

When it comes to English writers, I think of Shakespeare's "Hamlet," "King Lear," and Marlow's "Dr. Faustus, Chinua Achebe and I identify myself with Hemingway's Santiago in tough situations. I have great respect for "Old Man and the Sea's conclusive lines, "Man can be destroyed but not defeated," which are very near Iqbal's:

"Ghulami main na kaam aati shamsheeren na tadbeeren.

Jo ho zauqe Yaqeen paida to Kat jati hain zanjeeren."

Introduction

Noam Chomsky, a twentieth-century philosopher of language, is of the opinion that "language is primarily a means of constructing thought; contrasting with the modern consensus that it is primarily a means of communication." The Urdu language, a mingled constitution of 70% Persian, 30% Arabic, and 10% Turkish, became the means of communication after the conquest of the Arab conqueror, Mohd.Bin Qassim. The Mughals bestowed patronage, but the expansion of the British Empire caused it to shrivel. Urdu speakers are all over the world, including the United Kingdom, Bahrain, Bangladesh, Germany, Guyana, Afghanistan, Fiji, Malawi, Botswana, and Mauritius, in addition to being the Lingua Franca of Pakistan and a sweet Hindustani of Indian Territory, Nepal, Qatar, Saudi Arabia, South Africa, and Thailand.

Globalization has made Urdu lose its ground in India and Pakistan. Previously, most Muslims found that the reserves of religion were in the Urdu language, but as the religious literature is now abundantly available in the English language, even that feeling vanished. Despite all this, one should remember that one's identity remains in protecting one's language. A great Jewish thinker, Lone Rosovsky, in his essay Path to Extinction, says, "When languages die, whole cultures die with them, and communities lose." England is the third home of the Urdu language. The Pakistani and Indian settlers wanted to shift the wealth of their language to the younger generation. Most of the Pakistanis had to depend for their kith and kin's education on the Montessori schools for contemporary education and rely on mosques and maulvis from India and Pakistan for the learning of the holy Quran and Urdu. In an interview, when Athar Farookui asked Ralph Russell, a reputed Urdu teacher and a scholar, about the future of Urdu in Europe, he replied, "In my opinion, the future of Urdu in Europe, especially in England, is not very bright." According to him, the trained teachers at Montessori schools inspired the children of the Muslims of Pakistan more than the traditional Indian and Pakistani teachers and maulvis, as the teachers in Montessori schools deal with children quite according to their psychology. As a result, the importance of mosques for Urdu learning decreased. We are forced to think whether Urdu is "moribund" language. As Jamie-Wheeler rightly pointed out, "a language that has no speakers is either dead or extinct. A language that is only spoken by the elderly and not by younger people is called "moribund." A language that has very few speakers is endangered." We, as common people, do much bother about the existence of our language, even if the government does. The situation of the dying language can be reversed if the government seriously steps to protect the language, as its identity lies in that of a community. As Krishna Murthy, Secretary of Sahitya Academy, writes, "The primary issue is not that of a language but its speakers. If a community and its way of life are preserved, its language will automatically survive their identity."

In order to lead an elite life, both the citizens of India and Pakistan started to turn their heads towards English. So, the younger generation is inclined more towards English. Observing the inclination of the younger generation, a doubt arises as to whether the language will survive. According to Rosemarie Ostler, in his essay "Disappearing Language Spring 2000," he writes, "The definition of a healthy language is one that acquires new speakers. No matter how many adults use the language, if it isn't passed on to the next generation, its fate is already sealed. Although a language may continue to exist for a long time as a second or ceremonial language, it is moribund as soon as children stop learning it."

The Urdu language is endangered as the Urdu-speaking population gradually shifts its loyalty to the English language. Every aspect of life, employment, and trade is dominated by the English language. As SN Barman, director of the Central Institute of Indian Languages, Mysore said, "A language's survival becomes threatened primarily if it is abandoned by its speakers. People may give up their language for various reasons: better social identity, upward mobility, or economic reasons. Often, political reasons play a part, though no Indian language has become extinct due to the imposition of state policy."

Though it is a bridge too far to entrench, we must be honest and work. Can we take advantage of this when the government, under the Directive Principles of state policies, arranges compulsory education for every child up to the age of 14 years? Unfortunately, we commit errors, as The Siasath Urdu Daily reported on July 28, 2010. "It's a matter of great sorrow that the Urdu elite, with the view of gaining certain political advantages, has been striving to organise seminars and conferences, but they have never put pressure on the government in any way for the organisation of Urdu education at the primary and secondary level.

The intellectuals of the world who find charm in the Urdu language have made an epic effort. BBC Urdu Services, Urdu Academy California members, Anjum Suhail from Voice of America, and others are behind these efforts because they recognise the importance of the language.

In India, the Siasath Urdu daily gathered the world's Urdu editors to meet the challenges of changing trends.

In December 2011, there was a world Urdu conference...to reflect on the ups and downs, as well as the challenges that Urdu journalism has faced.

Anjumane Furoghe Urdu and Rajisthan Urdu Academy in Rajisthan expressed grave concern about the deteriorating situation in Urdu.

The Jammu and Kashmir Academy protested the UGC's failure to print. Even though many postgraduate students would come from Jamia Millia New Delhi, which was founded with the sole purpose of protecting Urdu and the interests of Urdu-speaking communities.

So far as a common man is concerned, he will be unaware of the loss if a language dies because he is concerned with his mere livelihood, which, according to the common man, will be food and accommodation. Andrew Woodfield, Director of the Centre for Theories of Languages and Learning in Bristol, England, suggested it in 1995. "The truth is, no one knows exactly what riches are hidden inside the least studied language," he continues, "but we have inductive evidence based on past studies of well-known languages that there will be riches, even if we don't know what they will be."

I acquired Urdu as my first language, as it is my mother tongue. I realize that it is the richest language for me. I must make use of its enrichments. Even though I did my post-graduate studies in English, I consider the degree to be a compliment. No need to be shy about saying this, a great language scientist says, that between the ages of 3–10, a child is the most likely to learn and grasp fluency. According to Chomsky, "Humans acquire language by unconsciously storing information in the brain which can later be used for many types of written and oral communication." After that, it is hard and even considered impossible, for the child to grasp the language completely. In this case, I am an exception.

I stake a claim that I am an aficionado of Urdu, but honestly, I am not. My devotion to Urdu is pretense. I am loyal neither to the community nor to the language. I send my kith and kin to English-medium schools, however costly the education may be. I crave their high-quality future and lustrous English tongue.

To be honest, only 10% of all English-medium children draw closer to the destination, where the parents persuade the children. Less educated and illiterate parents who leave everything to chance and rarely attend their children's school or monitor their academic growth suffer a severe setback.

We should take up this mission to protect and promote the awesome language to which we owe so much without much hype?

Slogans are futile. The occasion necessitates a panacea.

There are about 1000 registered Urdu magazines and papers. Instead of silly excuses for not subscribing, can we subscribe to a few with our little income? Can we have representation in Urdu in government offices? Can we take membership in libraries and make libraries enhance the number of magazines they have? Can we ask the librarians as members to shift the Urdu section from a secluded cobweb corner to a safer place where an Urdu reader can have access to Urdu books? Can we keep an eye on how Urdu-medium schools perform? Can we revive the publication of college magazines as the trend is almost dead? It certainly encourages students, breeds literary aptitude, and enhances their level of linguistic competence. Can we regularise teachers? Can we try to standardise the irregular curriculum design? Can we help schools form libraries? Can we provide computers and Urdu software? Otherwise, how can we alert the community to our rights? Will there be any sense in lamenting the ailing situation of Urdu-medium institutions unless we plan to take steps to rectify the lapses? Can we be a little bit audacious and prompt Urdu academies to be transparent and avoid helping plagiaristic materials get printed?

Are we struck dumb?

It is imperative to speak.

Let's have burning earnestness, vigorous action, and all the devotion of enthusiasm.

In the words of Faraz

"Aake ab tasleem karlen too nahin to main sahi,"

"Koun manega ke hum main se bewafa koi nahin."

Can a state or state authorities bear grudges against any language or its subjects? No, it cannot and should not. If it isn't considered a dox, I remember when we were in eighth grade, we were made stand on a cold morning to welcome an authority whose friend happened to be our teacher. After three hours of waiting, he passed through our school, and when our teacher quickly headed up the car garlanded him and gave him a representation, he said, "Don't lead your community cower, you have to follow the present trends. We were innocently raising slogans for the long life of the leader and his party. No, I don't blame the authorities for our handicapped situation, but I feel:

Mere jalte Makan ko kya maloom:

mere ghar ke charagh mujrim hain

It's a fact that even the patronage of the government cannot help a language flourish until people speak it and unless it becomes a source of employment.

My intentions are not to take a swipe at any organization, but rather to save our mother tongue from extinction. Those who take the responsibilities of supporting the language retain its status, stick to the posts for three years of tenure or more and play the lime and spoon race. Do all the participants win? No! Participation is much more important. But in fact, those who participate in the game with meraki will certainly win or at least be close to the winners. If the purpose of occupying the chair is not to chair the functions as a chairperson and be garlanded for getting lauded for being verbose, they can serve. Soon after occupying the chair, they turn their eyes blind to the requirements of the audience. They never test the waters and apprise the rulers of the needs of the audience. They are the votaries of the rulers. Do they have any zeal to serve and promote the language? Simply no. It is said, "zeal without prudence is frenzy."

Introduction To the Writers

Rashidul Khairi

Hyderabad Deccan is a cradle of great literary figures. Before Vali Deccani, Daagh it was Quli Qutub Shah who wrote about fifty thousand poems. There were great numbers of fictionists. The selections for translation are very careful. The intention behind this is to introduce Urdu fictionists to the outer world and to the younger generation of Deccan and India, who were deprived of learning the sweet language mostly by the lovers of the language, whose medium of instruction was Urdu and who earned bread in the name of Urdu. I was one among them. I know we sloganeered and never worked for it. One of the most prominent names of Urdu in the genre of novel-writing, Rashida Khairi was born in 1868 in Delhi. His father's name was Abdul Wahid who worked in Hyderabad. His predecessors were associated with the Mughal emperors as their teachers. Also, Deputy Nazir Ahmad was the uncle of Rashidun Khairi.

Rashidul Khairi's father died when he was very young, so the task of his upbringing fell on his grandfather. His uncle also continued to help. He studied Arabic, Persian and Urdu at home according to the customs of the time, but later entered an English-medium school. Upon the completion of his education, he took up a government job in 1891 and remained associated with it. When he retired in 1910, he began writing and gave many valuable novels to Urdu literature. He died at the age of 68. That is, he died in 1936.

As told above, Nazir Ahmad was a huge influence on Rashidun Khairi. Nazir Ahmed made women's reform the subject of his novels. Under his influence, Rashid al-Khairi drew attention to women's issues and tried to cover topics not only in his novels but also in articles that were based on the situation and reform of women at that time.

Mohiuddin Quadri Zore, Ph.D.

He was born in 1905. He was a distinguished writer, scholar, and linguist. He revived and gave new life to the Urdu language and literature. He had deep knowledge of Deccan history and culture. He was deeply involved in Sufism. He has translated the Dewan of the King Poet of Hyderabad, Mohammed Quli Qutub Shah. In the story Fourteen Pomegranate Seeds The professor put all the chapters and verses together. Hyderabad is a great state that was ruled over by highly talented kings, so it is very famous throughout the world.

Abul Hasan was called Tana Shah by his spiritual teacher, Hazrat Syed Shah Raziuddin. Hazrat Shah Raju Qattal lineage was the eighth after Sufi Hazrat Banda Nawaz Grau Daraz Kaliburg (Gulbarga), Abul Hasan has got nick name of Tana Shah from his spiritual teacher. Abul Hasan was a great statesman. There was peace and communal understanding during his period. Hanamakonda residents Akanna and Madanna were great Telugu poets, and they were the ministers in his reign. He had a great taste for architecture and music.

Hijab Imtiyaz Ali

November 4, 1906 – March 19, 1999.

Hijab Imtiyaz Ali was born on November 4th, 1906, in Hyderabad. She was educated in Arabic, Urdu, and music. She started writing for various magazines. She used to go by the pen name Hijab Ismail. Most of her works were published in Tahzeeb-e Niswan. She has written several stories and novels. Her present story, "Her One Hand was cut", reminds us of Coleridge's Rhyme of the Ancient Mariner, where the speaker of the poem coined the term, "Suspension of Disbelief."

Aziz Ahmed.

Aziz Ahmed was born on November 11th, 1913. He did his MA at Osmania University. He was a Pakistani-Canadian academic. He shifted to Pakistan after the country was divided. He was a poet, novelist, and translator. He translated many English works into Urdu. His present story is "Double Life," which deals with the character of a lady who was not what she posed. The love of the protagonist was not properly responded to. Of course, love is an experience and not explained, but it could be reckoned.

In the words of John Keats in La Belle dame sans Mercy, "She look'd at me as she did love,

And made sweet moan."

An unfair, merciless lady who neither allows him to live nor die.

It is neither a worldly love nor a divine one.

When the protagonist understood the reality that the woman he loved didn't want to invest in her emotions, he shed his thoughts as it was just like beating a dead horse, and so he became infallibly cheerful.

In the words of Ghalib,

"Wafa kaisi kahan ka ishq jab sar phodna tahra

To phir sange dil tera hi sange aastan kiyun ho."

Awaz Sayeed, 3 March 1933–1955.

Awaz Sayeed was educated at Anwarul Uloom. He worked for the Food Corporation of India after graduating. He wrote about seven books. Six of them are short stories, *Sai Ka Safar* (1969), *Teesra Mujasamma* (1973), *Raat Wala Ajnabi* (1977), *Kohe-Nida* (1977), *Benaam Mausamon Ka Nauha* (1987), and *Kuwaan Aadmi Aur Samandar* (1993), and a book on *khake* (personality sketches) called *Khake* (1985).

Loneliness is a state of mind, a perception, an unrelenting feeling. If we have intimacy with people, if we are not engaged at a superficial level, we cannot avoid it. The sadness is tempered by the anxiety. In old age, we are thewless. We want a convivial environment and want to be cared for by those whom we instinctively and tenderly care for. It is simply difficult to live swimmingly at this age. Unfortunately, the children, content with abandoning their parents, seek employment. The question is whether it can be indemnified.

Of course, the wealthy can hire workers to care for their parents. The question is whether they will serve their purpose, and the answer is simply no. Swami Vivekananda says, "A man should serve like a master," and the maids can never serve like masters. If we take the case of parents, they seldom depend upon the aid or maid to look after the children. This problem is explored by many other writers, like Jeelani Bano. Qamar Jamali but Awaz's face more like a wet weekend. Are the people who stay with their parents to look after them and be content with what they get here? Are they dying or starving to death? No.

It is difficult for the old generation to accept the tendencies of the new generation. The younger generation wishes to roam the world like the birds do, without any patriotic feelings and without home sickness. They prefer to stay in their old homes, though not as posh and convenient as the homes the younger generations live in.

Tabish khair says:

Refusing to be weeded out from this skyscraping street,

Where two people had grown roots, once scattered seed.

And now, with a hope stubborn as weeds,

Still peer through curtained windows when the gate creates.

Loneliness is the fate of the man of this age. R S Thomas writes in his poem, 'The Lonely Farmer' who has an overriding sadness.

Along a lane in spring, he was deceived

By a shrill; whistle coming through the leaves;

Wait a minute, wait a minute-four swift notes;

He turned, and it was nothing, only a Thrush

In the thorn bushes easing its throat.

He swore at himself for paying heed,

The poor hill farmer, so often again

Stopping, staring, listening, in vain,

His ear betrayed by the heart's need.

Iqbal Mateen

Iqbal Mateen is a great literary figure, born on February 2, 1929, in Hyderabad. He stands among the stalwart writers of the Deccan, like Maqdoom Mohiuddin, Dr. Raj Bahadur Goud, Dr. Hussainy Shahed, Syed Mohd Jawad Razwi, and Sulaiman Areeb. His first book, "Ujli Parchayyan," won him a great name. It was published in 1960. He won the Sahitya Academy Award. His present selection "Bare Wounds," crafts the character of the personal life of two harried employees who face a financial crisis every month. Either their big families are the recipe for disaster or the meager amount they earn as salary. The income and the expenditures seem to have no tally. Every first brings him a bad situation, making them eat dust, and they seem to have failed in satisfying the needs of his wife and children, so they face their ire. Jitender, who presents himself to be affluent, in fact had the same financial crisis but doesn't express his conditions before friends. It's a satire on the living conditions of government employees who can hardly meet both their ends and the financial crisis gives them a hard time. It hints at the lives of the people soaked up in poverty and the involvement of cocky money lenders in the lives of mediocre families. Can it be considered a person's moira?

Wajida Tabassum

Wajida Tabassum hailed from Amravati, Maharashtra. She was born in 1935. She secured graduation and postgraduate degrees from Osmania University. Her usage of literary devices like Aporia hyperbole, similes, and metaphors keeps a reader spellbound. Sometimes they look extreme and exaggerated. "Tabassum's fiction explores the microcosm of the home and the brothel. She focuses on the interiority of her protagonists, diving deep into the lives of Muslim women, occupying aristocratic spaces as begums, courtesans, mistresses, and domestic help." Aditi Upmanyu in her tweets writes on 7th, December 2021.

Her story, "Nau Lakha Haar," is full of metaphors and references to detonation of Hiroshima Bomb over Japanese. Most of the time, she gives morals in her stories. For example, her " Range Pairahen" is a wonderful lesson for people who spend their time dating instead of giving time to their own wives. The writer finds fault with the affected manners opted by aristocrats, but as a matter of fact, the stories are the atrocities caused against women when they are deprived of having sexual relations with their men by means of castration of men or when they are neglected, and their emotions are being ignored keeping themselves involved in external affairs. What's the cause of the protagonist women who were in neglection, who inveigle servant by saying "Haur Zara Ooper" or son in-law saying, "I wore the Nau Lakha Haar again?" She was deprived of her right to stay with her husband and her thirst remained unquenched.

I read her stories from the perspective of the atrocities against women, Atrocities or misbehavior against women are not limited to aristocrats; we can see political leaders, famous actors, or presidents of big countries exploiting women as well. Atrocities are not limited to particularly aristocrats. They are caused by even common man and even labour. The worst example is the "Nirbhay' case, or the case of three auto drivers who caused the death of a veterinary doctor.

Recently, the movement "Me too" exposed many so-called "sober" big personalities who belonged to the fields of journalism, filmmaking, and music. The men seem to refute the allegations. Most of the time, a woman is Hester Prynne, wearing a symbolic Scarlet Letter "A" and bearing humiliation while Arthur Dimmesdale-like men roam freely, denying all charges against them. Wajida Tabassum never condemns a woman. In "Utran" The maid's attitude against her lady was supposed to be a wild justice. She is righteous in pointing out the superficial religious attitude where a community uses the principles of religion partially or superficially for its own purpose. Religion is for the betterment of humanity. We abused the principles for our own pleasure ignoring the warnings and fear of hell. The man doesn't understand that the rules of the road are not for the roads but for the travelers.

In the current story, "Zakat" she exposes the follies of a particular duke's social behavior, and she exposes Bovary of the nawab. Depiction of the hollow boasting and misuse of religious principles that were propounded to be functional in out-of-the-ordinary situations.

Jeelani Bano

Jeelani Bano is one of the greatest literary figures of this century. Her writing covered the grief-stricken situations of human life and particularly those of have not's. This short story is a compact of her observations of human life in our region. She discovered poverty, atrocities against women, and injustices against the poor in this. The bomb blast is a sign of the action taken by the affluent to remove the poor. It was undoubtedly blasted in the faces of the poor or labourers to vacate the land for the construction of some magnificent structure. Munni describes the harsh realities of life and the teacher's becoming helpless and unable to defend her as the odd situation of the bomb blast, which was not less than doomsday and which made a perfect and mature man tremble. This story revolves around the Arabic teacher who used to scare mischievous children with the thought of hell. The students tell him that the hellish situation he describes is not different from the situation in their houses. Then they hear a bomb being blasted and fire spreading all over. The teacher asks God, when he has created hell in the world itself, where should I take them for heaven?

Mahshar, Masood Mirza

I happened to talk to Janab Masood Mahshar Sahab on the phone, and we also had a conversation on WhatsApp chat. "My stories comprise the social evils in the Muslim community," he said as he sent me his book, "Khushk Zameen Ke Phool." In his foreword, he writes, "Literature is the mirror of society." If literature doesn't harmonize with society, it doesn't last long. "Yes, he targets social evils in the Muslim community and suggests measures to improve them. The community must beef up and should be ready to square off. His' The King Makers "is a satire. It depicts the life of the Muslim community below the poverty line. Make hay while the sunshine lasts. Afterwards if you break head walls, there is no gain. The race, whose account of bravery and valour passed through the scorching deserts, roamed in the east and the west and scripted it in golden words on the chests of mountains, seraglios, streams, and waterfalls, bites the dust now owing to its desultory. Its lethargy and diffidence are the recipes for disaster. The maelstrom in the behaviour of a community is the skeleton in the closet. The powerful character that existed once upon a time and is now almost extinct, as the steadiness or the qualities he had frayed at the edges. The precarious situation in the lives of his sons and daughters is a typical fall of the Muslim community from up to down. One's somnolent attitude can be held responsible for this statis, the authors themselves are responsible. We are tin-eared and, knowingly or unknowingly, we turned a blind eye to our weaknesses and so fell flat. Regarding the leaders and their speeches, it can be said, "the blind lead the blind." In a democratic country, even a cobbler is also a king maker, but pronouncing a claim is undue.

Qamar Jamali

Qamar Jamali a great literary figure soon after independence appeared in the sky of literature of Deccan, she was born on April 02nd 1948. Her short stories and novels are a great edition to enrich Urdu literature... Her first short story was published in the year 1969 in a leading Urdu monthly magazine - 'Beeswin Sadi' (Delhi - India). She is the recipient of many awards like 'Qamar Raees' award in 2011, "Alambardaran-e-Urdu' award in 2017, 'Ismat Chugtai' award in 2018 to name a few.

She writes in her preface to SOHAB, "My stories are my identity. As Jogenderpal hopes she has really paved a path for the readers to probe life and its complexities, its realities. Her characters successfully create hopes in the readers. Most of his stories comprise his observation. On such story is in my selection for translation. Bonfire is Qamar Jamali's observation. When I had talk with the writer, she told me that the leper was a living character who used to sit before her office and gaze at people with longings the writer gives a realistic description of his harborous desires and that how leper feels When his bridges are burnt.

Prof. Baig Ehsas

Professor Baig Ehsas real name is Mohammed Baig. He was born on August 10th, 1948. In Hyderabad. He was a fictionist, a critic, and an orator. He has written modern short stories. He has served as the head of the Urdu department at Osmania University and the Central University of Hyderabad. He has been the mentor of many M.Phil. and Ph.D. research scholars. His present story, Dakhma, is a fantastic descriptive story where he painfully narrates the changes that occurred due to the division of the states based on language. Due diligence indicates that these two cultures have a lot of difference. It was like oil and water.

They cannot easily coexist due to fundamental differences in personality and opinion. The ludicrous changes in the city awaken poignant memories of the happier days of the writer's childhood. The unplanned construction of buildings will have a pernicious effect on local citizens. The affluent or the kings; family cannot thwart the impact. The crass benefited, and the courtly suffered.

Mohd Bahadur Ali

Mohammed Bahadur Ali is a leading literary figure in Telangana. He started writing stories at a very early age. He won first prize when he was in graduation previous for his story "Gahna", in "the Jyothi" Magazine of Arts and science college Subedari Warangal, once affiliated to Osmania University in 1966, when Professor Mughni Tabassum was the Chief editor. 'Honahar barva ke chikne chikne pat, "A thriving plant has tender leaves." Now one of his books, "Urdu Novel, Technique, Tahreek-o-Rujhanat" is one the reference book for research scholars in Ranchi University.

He received his postgraduate degree in political science from Aligarh Muslim University and Saifia BhopaL. He did his M.A in Urdu and has a doctorate from Osmania University. He is a postgraduate in history from Osmania.

Is compromise a sign of defeat? Wendy Moon Housten writes in Quora Digest... "But I feel it is a sign of maturity in most scenarios." Phyllis Antebi, in her Ph. D thesis, writes,

"Compromise is most often practical, mature, and offers lasting good will." In this story, the writer wants to point out the inconsistency of the mind. The mind that accepts the pleasures of life also must accept the pains. One must take the bitter with the sweet. Pain and pleasure go hand in hand. Those who accept only delight and not annoyance have a weak mind set, and such ingrate people prove that they are incapable. As it is well said, 'No rose without a thorn'; life is not a sashay (a journey taken for pleasure). It's not all moonlight and roses, most of the times it's full of knotty problems. Sameena commits a gaffe, but wisely decides to come back home.

Mazharuzzaman khan

The writing of Mazharuzzaman Khan reminds me of T.S. Eliot's Waste Land and F.R. Leavis phrase, "Vision of Desolation of Spiritual Draught.". Mazharuzzaman Khan looks to have cognoscenti in religious mythology. He suggests that the superpowers are unnecessary in the affairs of the Islamic countries and their involvement in the changing trends of the Islamic countries from Islamic to unislamic is rather unethical too. The oppression of the Palestine and the indifference of the claimant of honesty prove itself to be dishonest. The right has lost its value, and the fraudulent has thrived. He reminds all the world and Christians, of especially the value of the holy Quran, which speaks of Christ. Burning it or tearing it in the face of the people is an indirect insult to their own messenger. He speaks of the collapse and deterioration of social, psychological, and emotional infrastructure. The establishment of 26,500 km and 170 km. NEOM may go counter to the purpose of all religions. Contentedness, patience, piety, and tolerance have disappeared. The Muslims look like Dr. Faustus who signed Mephistopheles' bond for worldly pleasures in exchange for the soul. Despite all this the writer is not hope less as he declares the appearance of the "sword was gleaming on the white Minars of Damascus. Its rays were illuminating the entire planet."

Mukarram Niyazi

These days, it is broached; do we owe anything to our parents? Of course, an answer comes, "No, there's no inherent obligation." Children's intension is not involved in their birth. It's the own volition of the parents, certainly. The story of the writer doesn't go on this track. He is not the proponent of this theory. Undoubtedly, the approach of his father, friend, brother, beloved, wife, and mother irritated him, but he did not escape from the fulfillment of all these responsibilities. This narration is not recrimination.

As opined by Shahed Hameed from Pakistan, Mukarram Niyazi is against mechanical ethics. In the conclusion, he arrives at the viewpoint that the parents need the children's support, and their expectations are right. In the words of Henri Ward Beecher, "We never truly understand parental love until we become parents ourselves."

Undoubtedly, the approach of his father, friend, brother, beloved, wife, and mother irritated him, but he did not escape from the fulfillment of all these responsibilities. This narration is not recrimination.

We came to know from the words of his wife that he had tided over his friends. He sent his brother to Dubai. He was home and hosed in sharing the responsibility of his father by arranging his sister's marriage. His irritation is natural, and his expectation of his son is equally natural. Etymologically, an obligation is an act or course of action to which a person is morally or legally bound, a duty or commitment. What is the implied meaning of this passionate quest? When parents become senior citizens, they are unable to maintain themselves on their own. To get relief, they need children's support. Is it the children's responsibility to care for their elderly parents?

Contents

Worship
Rashidul Khairi 1

The Fourteen Pomegranate Seeds
Mohiuddin Quadr Zore, Ph.D. 11

Her One Hand Was Cut Off
Hijab Imtiyaz Ali 17

Double Life
Aziz Ahmed 24

6-Bare Wounds
Iqbal Mateen 36

The Blind Well
Awaz Sayeed (March 1933–1955.) 42

Zakath
Wajida Tabassum 48

In Search Of Heaven
Jeelani Bano 60

King Makers
M M Mahshar 65

Bonfire
Qamar Jamali 72

Tower Of Silence (Dakhma)
Professor Baig Ehsas 81

Changing Moments
Bahadur Ali 96

The Last Stage Of The Period Of Temptation
Mazharzzaman Khan 102

In Search Of You
Syed Mukarram Niyazi 112

Worship

Rashidul Khairi

Mohsin was atypically simple. He was an Islamic scholar, but he was not like today's Islamic scholars. He was a genuine scholar with a mind free of hypocrisy and other vices. He was unacquainted with frills and unaware of today's world. After completing his Islamic studies, he spent the whole day studying the knowledge of either the Holy Quran or Hadiths. He was hardly twenty-three, but his shape was highly Islamic. His thick and wide beard made him look like a complete man. Since he had heard that his parents were trying to engage him in marriage, he was extremely happy. He used to keep quiet at home, but when he's on the road, he would stop, and when he was out and came to know that marriage discussions were going on, he used to come home seeking some excuses, and hear the sisters and elderly women enquiring about his marriage, and when they took the bride's name, he was as keen as mustard. He felt pleasure and couldn't stop himself from burst with joy. Thus, he ate, slept and breathed marriage proposals. Mother and the guests were also busy all day with domestic tasks, but at night after nine o'clock there were sittings where they would vote on various proposals. The impact of this marriage description was such on Mohsin that he started coming home after the Isha (night prayer) or he used to sit in the mosque up until 11 o'clock or more and repeat the incantations, the hadiths, and the Holy Quran. For fifteen to twenty days, he returned at ten a.m., shortening his prayers and performing only farz (obligatory), excluding the namaz prescribed by the Holy Prophet (sunnah namaz) and supererogatory prayers (nafils). When he noticed the women leaving discussions after ten, he started evading even the obligatory namaz (Farz Namaz).

He would hurriedly perform the obligatory namaz and returned home, hiding his shoes under his arms. Finally, by Allah's grace, the relationship was styled, and marriage took place. Mohsin's father didn't see anything in this match except that the girl should say her prayers regularly. So, of all the proposals, one was given consent, and Mr. Mohsin became the groom and husband of a wife.

The first five and a half months flew by. All were happy that they had been blessed from every side by the Almighty. Habeeba, his wife, was an angel, not a woman. Panjsurah Darud Shareef (invoking God's blessings on the Holy Prophet) offered all kinds of prayers with beads reading half the night, and prayer continued until ten o'clock in the morning. Thus, in every matter, God's name and prayer were involved and nothing else. But after a few days, Mohsin understood the result of his prayers. The prayers cause inconvenience and difficulties for him. After the death of his father, he was hired as a teacher at the school. The superintendent was so strict that even for a fifteen-minute late arrival, he would ask the employees for an explanation, and here, the wife didn't leave namaz till ten. School timings were complete for seven and a half hours; it would be like fasting without blessings. For four and a half days he tolerated this, but at last he had to say, "It's better to arrange for some food as I remain hungry the whole day." His wife would say, "Should I drop off prayers for your food?" "Heaven forbid, how can I say this?" Mohsin would reply.

"But you are asking me to do that," the wife said. "Ma'am, say prayers in the night. "He used to reply. "I say night prayers all night and day prayers throughout the day." She used to quip.

"Do some of morning's prayers in the night itself." Mohsin said. "I am a Muslim." I must die and face Allah. "I can't leave Allah for your sake." wife would reply. "So, you want me to die of hunger the whole day?" when husband asked, wife would reply, "Nothing would happen against Allah's wishes." "Ma'am, please limit some of the prayers." Mohsin would request. His wife continued, "Wonderful, you asked me to minimize my prayers. What I recited after all a surath of Yaseen Shareef, a surath of Muzammil Shareef, a surath of Baqar, a surath of Yousuf, and Panjsurah in the morning are what I do besides this. I used to recite the whole holy Quran in a day. Now, after marriage, I couldn't do much."

"Then you propose a solution." Mohsin asked.

"You keep fasting every day." She spoke. His heart skips a beat.

"If I don't feel courage," Mohsin asked.

She said, "God will give courage."

"God helps!" he said, perplexed.

"It means I should leave incantation." Wife said. "Heaven forbid, how can I say that?" Husband said. "But what are you asking me to do?" wife said.

"Please recite in the night." The husband said.

"I recite the incantation for the night in the night and the recital for the day in the day…" wife said.

"Recite the day's incantation also at night," Mohsin said.

Days were passing. Mohsin couldn't fast regularly but met the conditions of fasting. Parents were looking for a regular praying girl to give their son a heavenly bootie in the world and thought they had found one. Had they lived a few more days to see how their son was living a heavenly life on earth? But neither of them lived to see it, and if not the father, his mother could have saved her son's life. It's not something Habeeba used to eat but didn't share with her husband. She was unconcerned about food or anything else; all she wanted to do was incantations. She was sure that Allah's condescension and forgiveness lay only in fasting. The malaria pandemic was sweeping through town at the time. Mohsin also picked up a temperature one afternoon. He reached home, panting for his breath. He covered himself with a blanket, but he couldn't control the shivering. When the shivering subsided, he asked his wife.

Mohsin said, "The upper division clerk stated that malaria affected all humans equally, but that Indians were more affected because they did not take precautions."

"No precaution can help. If one is fated to suffer from any disease, millions of attempts would go in vain." Wife replied. The argument continued in the same vein. Mohsin said helplessly, "that is correct, ma'am; careful thought is also required, along with a person's fate. Mohsin said, "Those who have loose bowels and keep their stomachs light, use Resochin, and keep houses mosquito-free by removing their larvae will never get malaria."

"Why had Basheerun teacher died?" wife questioned. "Ma'am, it was a coetaneous abscess that killed lady teacher Basheerun." Mohsin said,

"They were the rainy days, whether it was a cutaneous abscess or tuberculosis." Wife replied.

"Ma'am, what can I do now?" "I am unable to move and reach the doctor." He said in obvious discomfort. It's season fever, like the chapatis of the fifteenth night of Rajab, the eighth month of the Islamic calendar. No house is free from it.

"Go to a doctor in the morning." Wife said. It was a seasonal fever. When the temperature subsided, Mohsin went to see a doctor in the morning. He gave him laxative medicine. Poor Mohsin took one day off from work and asked his wife to provide him hodgepodge at 12 o'clock. But then she completed the Ishraq prayer and started a prayer book, forming an impregnable fortress around the house. Mohsin was hungry when he noticed his wife sitting on the janamaz, busy with her prayers. With a lot of willpower, Mohsin realised the true value of a pious wife. He exclaimed indignantly, "So you want me to observe fasting even in this state?" He felt peeved. "Hmmm... hmmm. "ma'am, you continue your prayers, I'll sleep. "Hmmm... hmmm...." When the wife finished praying, it was already 1 o'clock, and the time spent preparing for cooking hodgepodge had already passed an hour. When Mohsin started taking it, the wife went for afternoon prayer. There was not enough salt in the hodgepodge. But who could he have asked to provide salt? He waited for four to five minutes and then got up to take some salt himself. When he went in the room, it was totally dark there. He groped for the salt and got chilies, coriander powder, onions, and garlic, but he couldn't get salt. When he was about to return, he collided with the wall, and it thundered. He held his head and sat there, spreading his legs. The wife was in deep in prayers, and the husband was dozing. There was no better opportunity for the cat to take advantage of. She ate the hodgepodge and the soup. This situation had been so bad that even if it were an angel, he would have lost his patience due to these continual tortures. After all, Mohsin was a human being. He was getting a little cocky now. His close friends and family advised him on some of the lessons and time had also taught him some lessons. Frowns and signs of irritation began to appear on the lips. But neither his laugh nor his anger impacted his wife. She was indulgent with her work. Though Mohsin got irritated, his wife didn't pay any heed to it. A time approached when heaven on earth became an example of hell for him. When her spiritual teacher, and he narrated him the whole incident.

Habeeba was also observing her husband's attitude. When she realised that her husband's presence was impeding her worship. She decided to go for the Haj pilgrimage. It was time for her to plan a Haj pilgrimage, and if not a permanent stay, she wanted to spend a year or two there. to get rid of this trouble. She knew well that her real uncle was going on the Haj pilgrimage, so for expenses, her gold ornaments disposal would be enough. The husband or anyone else couldn't interfere in this issue. So, it happened. Mohsin couldn't dare to go against the intentions of his wife. The days neared, and Habeeba started packing her luggage. When her uncle came to ask about Mohsin, he expressed nothing but silence. So, he agreed to take her with him. She handed over her jewelry to her uncle in the presence of her husband to sell it, and he sold it. It happened on Thursday. On Friday, Habeeba went out after Friday prayer for meetings. She stayed at her mother's house that evening and went to see her spiritual teacher on Saturday. He had already heard the details from Mohsin and knew about the facts. He called for her. When the husband and wife sat near the spiritual teacher, he asked Habeeba whether she sought her husband's permission to go on the Haj pilgrimage. Habeeba quipped, "Yes, no Muslim denies permission for such a noble cause." The religious leader said,"This is not a right criterion. Why can't one deny permission?" If it had been so convenient, the whole world would have gone to Hajj. There are some unusual situations and circumstances, but everyone has the right to express their opinion until they are prohibited from doing so. He is your husband. If he doesn't permit you wholeheartedly, you cannot go, and your pilgrimage will not be accepted."

Habeeba said, "Certainly he will suffer if I go." The spiritual teacher said, "You know it well; then how can you intend to go? You couldn't properly understand a Muslim's Allah. I never meant to say that Muslims' God is different, but I want to say that you didn't quite understand Islam. As far as our relationship with God is concerned, it's for the betterment of worldly life, not religion for religion's sake or prayer for prayer's sake. What happens if a man dies on a hill, he leaves the world, reciting the name of Allah. No. As a wife, be obedient to him. He understands and supports your difficulties and problems. It's his duty to keep you happy, and your duty is to keep him satisfied. This is real prayer; this is real pilgrimage. If you die keeping him happy, I assure you that your Haj pilgrimage is complete. I hear that you are so indulged in recitations and incantations that you don't care for your domestic responsibilities. You would rather say prayers than serve your husband. You let your husband suffer from hunger, but you make no change in your routine incantations. This is not a preparation for heaven; rather, it's a preparation for hell. You have spoiled your husband's peace by shirking your responsibilities and seek God's approval. You are defaming Islam, and you are not a good example for others to follow. I am saying that your example is unacceptable and should not be followed, as it is harmful. By doing so, you are becoming a recipe for disaster. You are damaging the human cause of Islam and committing a sin. Don't you remember what Prophet Mohammed instructed a day and night worshipper to do—what the prophet used to do? It means to complete worldly duties, fulfill your worldly responsibilities, and say prayers. Don't eschew prayers. Did the prophet Mohammed peace be upon his soul and his companions sideline worldly responsibilities? Your heaven lies in the service of your husband. It is your duty to keep your husband happy, and he should keep you happy without detaching yourself from worldly responsibilities. Or one man's meat is another man's poison. Islam doesn't advocate this. I pass a verdict that if you go like this without the consent of your husband, you and behave like a hidebound. It's surefire, God will not accept your pilgrimage. I understand if the circumstances favour Mohsin, he will not pass up the opportunity to perform Haj. You two can work well together." The spiritual teacher's talk inspired Habeeba, but some ingrained habits were difficult to root out. Over the course of a year, she decreased her incantations gradually and made Mohsin's services her prime objective. After paying attention to her responsibilities, she would concentrate on saying prayers, and Mohsin had no protest over this. He was happy that his wife was performing his religious tasks and equally concentrating on him. Mohsin was not a poor man. He was affluent to some extent, but until she was busy with incantations, skipping her domestic duties, the peace was ruined. Biryani and sour-sweet rice dishes were worse than dal and sauces as they were not prepared with concentration. Sometimes when Mohsin needed water, the morsel was stuck in his throat, and the wife was reading beads unconcernedly. The change not only ended Mohsin's difficulties but also made Habeeba realised her mistakes. Muslim women are not merely meant for incantations and prayers and should not be unaware of worldly responsibilities. It should be noted. One day when it was raining cats and dogs, Habeeba said, "It's already ten; the rain is not ending; what to cook is a question." I think the besan flour is there; make its bread. "The cook also didn't come today." Mohsin said. Habeeba got up, kneaded flour, and prepared bread. After all, it was only for two people. When the people were sitting and about to start taking bread, the spiritual teacher appeared. Habeeba tried to get up, but the teacher asked them not to get up and eat together. There was bread, garlic sauce, and mango pickles on the dining cloth. "I came here and was held up due to the continuous rain. I am happy to see you both eating together. This basin bread is better than the biryani and sour-sweet rice dish. "And Habeeba, this service you are extending to your husband is far better than your prayers."

The Fourteen Pomegranate Seeds

Mohiuddin Quadri Zore, Ph.D.

"What a mellifluous voice is coming!" The king of Golkonda said, putting his signature on the last piece of paper. The drawing room of 'The Dad Mahal' abounded with the elegant upper crust and the well-behaved servants. The king's attire, the embellishment of the colorfulness of carpets, embroidered curtains, the observation of the throne etiquettes of the well-mannered affluent, courtly manners, and the readiness of servants revealed glimpses of extraordinary sincerity in every manner and matter.

When Madanna wrapped up all the papers and when the king got relieved from the unnerving writings, he looked astonished at the magnificent gathering.

During this, the mild sound of a melodious song was continued. "What a canorous voice this is!" A question came from his mouth again. Meer Bakhshi said, bowing down with folded hands respectfully. My patron, "Dhamis, is being attributed to the 'Chadar Mahal' cistern. "This is the sound of the songs of peacocks and peahens. "

"How convenient it is to make consistent hard work a luxury!" the king said, accepting the salutations of the lords. He went up a storey. His intimate people escorted him. "And my lord, the rhythmic cadence of it is so pleasing that one who joins in will be with great gusto." A trusted person came near and intimated him slowly.

"You might get pleasure from the dance yourself."

The king said, laughing.

The colourful buildings were seen on the palms from the upper storey, and in the middle of it, the crystal water of the huge cistern was a crackerjack, reflecting the last of Qutub Shahis' miraculous constructions. "How fast this palace was readied." "The king said jubilantly." "We will very soon shift into it."

"My lord will certainly be delighted with that dance." One of the true blues came near him and told him.

Your mind is always occupied with it. If you wish, arrange it tomorrow. "The king turned to him and said,

The next day, they were preparing for celebrations. A marvelous, rhetorical, sky-touching 'Char Mahal' became a spectacular show on the bank of the Musi River, raising citizens' eyebrows. Every arch of it was frabjously sparkling. The great cistern was brimmed with pellucid water. Arrangements of lights and crackers were made to make celebrations gussy. The dancing picture of the image of colourful lights presented a glorious scene.

A glossy white ship abutted to broad stairs was waiting for the king. The adornment with seashells dotted on it and the silver sheets covered around it presented the look of diamonds and pearls when they reflected the rays of light. The nimble, aureate punk women in uniformly dressed Tashkent bodycon stood there like faeries, stood there in the row of the lights with their wings spread. The high-born nobles and genteel and polite women seemed to be drowning in the river of jealousy.

Their fortunes were going to favour them with a precious Tashkent dress and a bag full of silver and gold, and it would be more than their entire life's earnings. The labourers of Golkonda were very fortunate; they would earn at the prime of their lives many rewards, and that is why they didn't take the name of work for a long time. As they were free from care for a long time and avoided working, it resulted in a scarcity of labour.

When the prayer of Isha ended and when the lamps were exhibiting their velour, there was uproar about the arrival of the king. The tent—pitcher rejigs the carpets and sees that there won't be any wrinkles on them. The bearers once again checked the lights. The people who were meant for burning crackers stood in one place, copacetic, like installed statues. The wanton, astute Tashkent-clad labourers were walking on the eggshells, adorning and arranging their garments in mirth, and feeling the blue sky because the king himself was arriving to see their performances. They wanted to ameliorate their performance.

The soldiers saluted the king outside the mansion. The still crowd began to move. It seemed as if due to some force of spell life infused in the lifeless puppets, the bursting of crackers, singing melodious songs and dhamis around the cistern commenced simultaneously. When the king was about to board the boat, the artificial plants, animals, and human beings of the colourful crackers began to move, and the marvy performance of Dhamis, twisting the waists of the girls' frenzied legs, was creating the picture of a zero bomb. The ecstatic young girls' golden dancing costumes were shining like the galaxy in the radiance of the movements, presenting the scene of thunderbolts at every step. The eye some cynosures' organs resembled refulgence parts, casting doubt on their being human-shaped refulgence.

The popular and favourite king of all mounted the boat and became engrossed in his thoughts. He was doing with forty winks. There was a peripeteia. A crony from his spiritual guide, a beggar in frayed pieces of clothing, an intimate friend of the days' straitened circumstances, appeared there during this merriment and called Tana Shah from Char Mahal gate. At this moment of merriment, the affluent and courtiers couldn't allow the appearance of the beggar. The on-duty squad stopped him at the gate. He was the one who was lost in divine meditation. He resisted the hurdle. The freemen hermits never liked limitations and hindrances. From there, he summoned his goombah. The king, Tanasha, was alarmed due to the calls of the Shah. He felt for "a moment, I took a nap and I saw my friend Chanda Shah in my dream." but again he heard the same call. From the gold laced dancing girls, the melodious song creators, the sounds of the crackers, the sounds of the bands from everywhere, he heard the same sound, "Tana Shah Tana Shah." He turned and saw his friend, Chanda Shah. At the corner of the cistern, the affluents and courtiers were forbidding him from calling.

The king's boat touched the bank. The beggar jumped on to it. The whole gathering had a blank look. The beggar took out a pomegranate from his chattel and said, "I am sent by my spiritual leader with an order that wherever I see you I should make you eat this whole pomegranate."

Abul Hasan embraced his friend, who was dressed in rags, and kept the pomegranate, sent by his spiritual leader on his eyes and head, extracted five seeds. When putting them in his mouth, he felt them sour. He dared not spit it out. He swallowed them with difficulty. The beggar did not remain silent and insisted on swallowing the entire thing. The king ate five seeds to show regard for his friend and his spiritual leader. The beggar insisted again. The king said, "Brother, you keep it here. I will eat it next time."

"What do you say?" Chanda Shah exclaimed, "Should I disobey the orders of my spiritual leader?" I will not commit such a sin. "

It was an internal affair of Chanda Shah and Tana Shah. They were like two peas in a pod. The magnates had nothing to interfere with. I didn't ask you to disobey the saint. I promised I would eat it afterwards. Now I am not inclined to eat it."

"Broh, I have been commanded to make you it, or return it." At least these four seeds are taken. I will seek Hazrat's permission to keep it with you to eat later. "

Fakir Shah went to Hazrath in a moment.

Hazrath saw Chanda Shah and asked him, "Has Tana Shah eaten a complete pomegranate?"

"Yes..."Yes, my lord, his health isn't good. He ate a few seeds and said he would eat the remaining seeds later. If your honour permits me, I will keep this fruit with Tana Shah, Chanda said trembling.

How many seeds did that unfortunate man eat?" He asked in rage.

"Yes... Five...Five...four...He ate fourteen seeds."

"Alas!" The Hazrat, the sortiger said with affliction. "He was fated to rule only fourteen years as a king."

Her One Hand Was Cut Off.

Hijab Imtiyaz Ali

I came out of the library on a steamy evening, after finishing one of my stories. I abruptly heard someone's footsteps thudding on the stairs of the garden s. The sound of someone's thuds on the stairs OH! God! Who was that Jonas?" I asked the old Negro woman wobbly with fear. But where was that deaf rat? Not certain. She did not answer. You know I am fond of reading the stories about ghosts. I stepped back with two thoughts, due to fear of either ghost or evil soul but fortunately I could see the image of the man who was coming. The image gave me heartsease, as it was our beloved Harley. I became restless to see him. I swished the curtain and hurried to the stairs, "My Harley, you appeared out of thin air." I uttered suddenly... "Why shatzi, why is your face pale like a lemon, what's the matter?" He said this and pulled me towards him with affection.

He gave her a big cuddle and told her not to worry. "Ah! What a pleasant moment! He was dressed in a black satin coat and white tie. The redolent whiff of 'One night in Cairo' came from his kerchief. I delayed in saying. "Yes, Harley I was afraid. Just now I wrote a story on ghosts, I came out finishing the story and heard the sound of your steps, I thought it was a ghost. In these eastern countries ghost appear frequently." He tapped my back and laughed in stentorian voice. "This girl is insane. Look! My life, you don't think more about souls God forbid, lest you may become a soul and dissolve in the air. Look how lean you are! Just like the first day moon." Hearing this I looked at my body in blue georgette which was looking like the blue flame of a candle. I smiled and said, "Harley my leanness is not a cause of any temporary ailment. I am way worn. You know I have a lean body right from the beginning. These days the difficulties of travel and forest camps made me more fragile besides this over and above The East forests and the heat of mountains. Look two hours have passed after sun set yet the hot waves are still prevailing in the garden." "Any moment gentle breeze will begin Roohi." Harley said. "In these hot countries a fascinating climate begins at 8 P.M. And a few minutes left to eight." He said and had looked on his watch. "If you want, I will come out with you for a simple walk." "Yes, Harley I myself fed up sitting in the library for a long time." I said this and I descended the stairs along with Harley and came to the garden. The moon light was prevailing, but its effect was stained by the electric lamps. A series of huge buildings were there at both the sides of the road. In a few minutes we reached the splendid building of a hotel 'For Caves'. Our eyes were dazzled due to the brightness of the electric bulbs. Its bloom slpendour was famous in the whole city.

I said, "Harley I like this place very much, whenever I come here for two days I stay here. I am tickled pink when I find life in every corner of this place. Harley raised his head looked at the building and said, "If you had come here five years back and stayed here, you would have screeched with fear."

"Why so...?" I asked and my curiosity increased. "Why would I let a shriek?"

"Yes darling," Harley said, "A strange event took place here, for the whole year this place is as resplendent as you see now, but on 21 November the hotel became appallingly deserted, then it won't remain a hotel but change into pyramid mummy chamber."

"Oh! God protect us." I kept my hand on my chest. "Why what was the reason?"

"Roohi a dreary event used to take place that date every year. I would make you feel jittery. You would feel weird and wonderful." He continued to talk, "That my friend and I put it to an end."

I was stunned and saw his face, "Harley you are talking like the stories of Arabian nights."

"Yes, my darling." Said Harley, with certainty. "I am not lying. You know my friend, Captain Feroz."

"Yes." I spoke.

"He was with me. We witnessed the incident with our own eyes...Come on Roohi. We shall sit there on a coach of the garden nearby. It's dark there, it gives more pleasure to describe and listen such event in the shades of the stars."

When I heard, I held Harley's beautiful hand and brisked away towards darkness like a soul. It was a natsukashii for me, I said, "Harley if the incident was that horrible and attention-grabbing, why didn't you write to me five years back? You are bad."

"How could I write such an incident when you were severely ailing and staying with your father on the bank of Shyok?"

He continued, "Moreover I almost forgot the incident. When you told me about the lively environment of the splendid hotel your words reminded me of the incident that this hotel used to turn into grave like one day, on 21 November before five years." While talking we reached orange tangerine tree and sat on a coach. The night winds harmonized with organum melody presented an ecstasy. The herbs let the ambrosial of buds of night queen. Ah! The night of separation in the past when the pleasant Asian warm night, when the ornamented crystal-clear sky was full of stars, when Harley was sitting beside me narrating stories. It was an onsra. Oh! God when would those days turn up"

"Give years back..." Harley started, "I came here along with Captain Ferozi. I was a green leaf in the military. We reached here on 20 November and intended to stay four days, but the manager told us that we could stay there with pleasure except on 21 November. We had to stay outside as the hotel would be cordoned off. I asked him to take it to be a hearsay. He said on 21 November this hotel was completely vacated, neither travelers stay here nor the service people. As many years back a heinous crime took place here. A helpless woman was murdered ruthlessly. This woman comes out of her grave on the 21 November night and roams in all the hotel rooms. It seemed she wanted to take revenge upon someone. When Ferozi heard this, he said we shouldn't be afraid a woman and especially of the helpless woman. The next day we went out to one of the towns for hunting. It was late when we returned. It was eleven when we returned the hotel. Everywhere there was grave like silence, loneliness and bleakness. No servants were there. The white moonlight took tall oak trees and guava tree in its arms. In the quiet night the leaves were susurrus in an orphic way. We realized it was 21st November of which the manager warned us...but the deer was in head lights. It was eleven there was no use going from here."

Captain Ferozi said and went to put on the lights of courtyard and relaxed after switching on the lights. I followed him. We were completely tired Roohi." He paused for a while and said,

"All of sudden a door of washroom was opened." When I heard this from Harley, the eldritch situation made me feel jittery. I looked at the darkness and shook with fear. The Cairo Night Aroma had struck a chord of that night and separation...He continued. "After a few moments we heard some kind of noise in the washroom. Suddenly Captain Ferozi said worrying, "look what is there in the washroom?"

"I was scared and turned my chair towards the washroom. A woman covered in white veil. Her arm was cut. I was dumb found. My eyes were shutting. I was nervous. After some time, the woman called me towards with hand's gesture and went towards the garden slowly. We acceded. She was turning and watching us frequently to be assured of following her. We were following her. She stopped silently under the guava tree. There was a spade under that tree. She indicated to the spade. My friend unwillingly took the spade and looked at her. When she was satisfied with what we were doing she asked us to follow her. She went towards the well. There she stood motionless under a small tree. She was waiting for us to reach her. When we reached, she earnestly requested with a gesture to dig the grave. She was young belle ame. Her face was expressing oppression. In the pale moonlight her face was looking heart rending. My friend started digging the grave. When he was tired, he relaxed for two minutes she requested with a queer eagerness, to do it soon, she looked fraught. While digging Feroz's spade touched something and he couldn't dig anymore, and said, "I can't dig anymore." he said this handed me over the spade. I put off my coat and gave it to Ferozi and started digging. A long stone was there inside. I took it and threw it out. She suddenly rushed towards the stone took it in her hand." "It was not looking like a stone, but like a bone." My friend said. "As I was about to reply, she moved slowly towards the other side of well and called us. We were in Dutch. lt looked something bad going to happen." Ferozi said. Harley continued, "The woman went there and asked us to dig there. I started digging the place where she indicated. When it was two feet deep, she forbade us to dig further. I stopped. We three were silently standing. The woman turned to the other side and was busy in doing something. What was the act if you come to know, you would tremble. The long bone which came out from the ditch, she took in her hands and was trying to join it to her arms. As if it were her hand. When the hand was joined with the remaining part of her arm, she looked at us, and entered her grave quietly, and vanished from out sight. It was axiomatic. We were flabbergasted. We fill her grave with soil. It was heard that since then, 21 November was never horrifying."

Double Life

Aziz Ahmed.

Finally, you wrapped your hands around my neck. The shoe is on the other foot now. I am surprised by this change. Imagine two years back. Who could have guessed that you would come to Delhi like this to meet me? I still remember once, when I asked you to take ice cream in Quality, you very politely replied that you didn't want to be seen with anyone in Delhi to avoid being impugned. I hope you remember I left movies in the theatres, mainly because you didn't like to come with me. How careful were you about "what men would say?" How careful were you about your status? How proudly you declared you were the only girl in the university about whom people didn't get a chance to wag their tongues. Isn't it ambivalence that despite your wish to meet me, you didn't do so, as you didn't want to become the talk of the town or lose your reputation for my sake, so you eschewed moving with me? You went off on a tangent. I am surprised at what happened to you today. What happened to your dogmas? You remember how you used to say that a man-woman relationship should be healthy and tidy? What happened to your philosophy? You used to say that you were a hard stone. This couldn't be waved away so easily. You declared yourself to be a stone on which the waves of passion collide and become still. You were as tough as old boots. It will not be daunted by hot or cold... The fact was that I didn't find the spark in your eyes, which I wanted to see. It was not sybaritic. Your smile was never an elegant one, which I desired to see. You lacked the ability to listen and gauge others' moods. You lack verve. Your eyes were like an unmoving sea where the silent ingratiation of my craving couldn't cause any tumult, nor my anxious eyes couldn't reach its depth. I failed to hog the limelight. You were queer. You were very queer. When you talked, you showered the flowers of affection. If you didn't want to, you made lame excuses and evaded for a long time. I couldn't guess whether I was tolerable or not. I couldn't forget our first meeting, despite it being entirely enterprising. I was remembered. When Mrs. Birlas introduced me to you, you caught my eye then. I was confident I am dishy. I would say you were not attracted. I could never accept the smile on your face as a ritual. Then I decided to come close and observe you, but on our second visit your attitude was so indifferent that I was ashamed and surprised. I realized I was judging a book by its cover. You were standing at the Kashmiri gate waiting for a bus. I passed by and offered you a lift; you smiled and declined, but this smile was different from the previous one. You were a lovely jolt, like a sharp-edged knife that could inflict serious harm if touched. After this, I was restless. You would laugh if I told you how restlessly sleepless, I passed the night. You knew it from the beginning that it would torture me. You know the ropes. You might have played this game purposefully. It gave a shock to my manly prestige. I wanted to leave you to your devices, so I put a lid on my passions. I didn't want to see you as a tin-eared lady in the future. I wish I were in a position to maintain my stand. I wish I were allowed to maintain the status quo. How different you were that day at the radio station. I was sitting in the waiting hall and was having a glance at my speech. I didn't see you coming. You looked bright eyed and bushy tailed. You came very close to me, greeted me with great warmth, and sat on the sofa. I was stunned to see your changed behavior. How well did you blend with me? That night, the radio staff was ingratiating you, but you didn't entertain them. Then my fate played a trick and put us on one track. We were reassigned to one hospital, and we started sitting together. I don't know its effect on you. But I was dead chuff to see the change. I thought I would be able to fight against your pride and fickle-mindedness and face black swan events to set us on the right track, but you were not inexperienced enough to be trapped. The whole day you used to make the charts of patients, and despite all my interest, I couldn't do anything. Many a time we got an opportunity to spare some time from work and talk, but very gingerly you avoided it and didn't provide me an opportunity to speak. Finally, being knackered with this, I started staying outside. Sometime in patients' wards and sometimes without other doctors in the laboratory. Apparently, you didn't understand this change in the beginning, but later you were close to home. Not bearing the change in my behaviour, you started complaining politely that I was staying outside, and you feared being alone. I replied that I was not of any interest as a source of entertainment for you, though, in being here. When I said this, you accepted it as a defeat, and it's worth a try to take care of downtime. You yourself said that it would make the work easier and that mental tiredness would also diminish.

Our talk started roving about hospitals, patients, doctors, politics, literature, philosophy, psychology, and music, and from there it turned towards our individual selves. From education, past life responsibilities, individual tastes, etc. were discussed. Then I started eating your tangerines and you started drinking tea from my thermos. The slow smile on your lips was replaced by a layer of dejection. Gradually, we started talking more and more. Voluble, you were a church bell. Whenever you got time, you used to occupy the chair beside my table and we both indulged in talk, and at last you accepted that you liked my talk and that whenever I was absent you felt bored.

Even with all our twitching, we can't get close. You were far from me. You used to use the adjective "clean" whenever you talked about friendship. This irritated me a lot. Why are you feigning? Why didn't you accept that we were men and women and that we liked each other? If so, what was hindering us? The academic shape of this friendship was not tolerable to me. I was maintaining it, thinking that your heart was also made of flesh like mine. And slowly, they would accept love. But how long...?

I beg to differ. One day, I got poked up with repetitive off-the-peg behaviour. I intrigued and told you that our friendship was a flirt. You got irritated as you thought I insinuated and told you that our friendship is above gender relations, so pure and so infallible. I told her how long we could deceive each other like this. Whatever A rose is a rose, whatever name you give it. Believe me, our relationship is not more than flirtation. Only one thing acts in our subconscious, and that is that we are men and women who are attracted to each other. Our emotions are pent up. You attuned me out as you felt annoyed with my talk. Where water is the boss, the land must obey. So, I changed the topic, thinking to let the sleeping dog lie.

I couldn't understand whether you were canting. If our involvement is so pure, why did you get offended by my relationship with Kaushaliya, Bimla, and Shama? To this day, my conscience censures me that, for your sake, I shoved aside all those four women. They were no less beautiful when compared to you. They also liked me, as you did. But the attachment with me had no academic name. They didn't want to play with my emotions. They were plain girls who found a man in me.

You were fond of Kaushaliya first. The truth is that your admiration for Kaushaliya created a place in me for her. But after Major Khan informed you that I was with Kaushaliya at the Chamsford club, you changed your mind about Kaushaliya. You started making fun of her loud talk. The clumsiness of her colour was apprehensive to you. Not only this, but also her college traditions were reaching out. Whenever you heard that I was seen with Kaushaliya, the colour of your face changed. You appeared different back then. The streaks of emotions were clearly observed on your ebony face. It's a different thing that those lines encouraged me a lot, and I thought your heart is also made of flesh like mine. It certainly throbs for me. Or why would you feel jealous of Kaushaliya? I listened to the tittle-tattle about her. You talked about the scandals of Kaushaliya. One day, you spoke to me about Kapoor and Kaushaliya's relationship. I was not hurt. I was enjoying myself instead. That day, how depressed you were! I am not a kid and not to understand it. I could understand the aim of your words and their reaction. I was sure that one day or the other, you would pluck the mask of healthy friendship, morality, and nobility from yourself being embarrassed, and appear in a genuine manner and take me in your captivating arms.

The most pleasant thing for me was that you quarreled with Bimla for my sake. That poor lady's love for you has no bounds. She knew my affection for you, and she honoured it. You were also convinced of her decency. You accepted she was as nice as nine pence. She was full of beans, a lighthearted daughter of Kashmir, bricky and quite open-minded like ice winds. Whatever she thought, she would speak outspokenly. She admitted her love for me, but she never tried to repel you from my heart in any way. She told me that she had been attracted to me ever since I came to Lahore to attend a radical democratic conference. My heat of firebrand speech had a similarity with that of the heat of volcano in her heart. She started worshipping me, but by that time you had overpowered me entirely. When Rajan knew about this triangle love, he was stunned. He told me that I had not just captured Bimla, I hadn't just captivated a tigress. The whole city was mad after her. This woman was a woman, a flame wherever it flared up. It burnt a few hearts. She had no idea what's there in you for which she was inclined towards you. One evening, when we were having dinner in Omar Qayyam, Bimla was also there with us. Your description came after someone expressed sympathy with me and called me unfortunate. It meant that you didn't mingle with us and appear with me in any program. Bimla repined and said, "His misfortune is like a wildfire which didn't extinguish after burning one but continued to lead to deterioration of the air quality and loss of property, crops, resources, animals and people." God knows how many innocent hearts are mourning for their misfortune, but they are helpless. That day, I got annoyed, and I was very angry with you. In fact, my pillow became wet with my tears. On the second day, I went to Bimla. She saw him grief-stricken and shed tears. And said, "If I caused you any pain, I apologize, but how long do I see you ruining like this?" No one has the right to manipulate your expectations. How come she couldn't come for an outing with you? I told her all the reservations you had in your mind, your etiquette, your fear of being seen and losing your reputation, and about the neat friendship without physical involvement. When she heard it, she jeered at me. I laughed. She knew a cat in gloves caught no mice. You have seen enough of the world, yet you are so innocent. Come to Shamshi's house today. I will show you what the world is like.

We went to the Western Court. Shamsi was our class fellow. Look, Mr. Romeo (she used to call me a romantic lover as a joke), we've arrived at the perfect time. You would have lost everything, had you come late. We started sipping tea. After a few minutes, she called me by the window. You know what I saw? You were sitting with Major Khan in his car. A disaster has befallen me. I got into a blue funk. Khan got down from the car and opened the door for you. You took his support to get down from the car, then moved hand in hand and ascended the stairs. I came back and sat in my chair. Despite my struggle, I couldn't grip myself. My heart sank into my boots. Bimla told me that you come here every evening with Major Khan, and from here you go to Roushan Club. She told me that we were invited by Shamshi to this club that day. That night, I saw how you were drinking. It was a new part of your life exposed to me. Why did you keep your relationship with Major Khan hush hush? I was devastated. I could hardly contain myself when I blurted out. My dreams were shattered. What was the double life? I read about it in books, but I didn't come across it. Today's live example of double life was before me. My emotions were being crushed in the mill of your double life. How suddenly I became despondent because of an undesirable event. I couldn't say and could dare to accept it. The situation was decidedly awkward. I didn't get that bad a defeat as I have now before Bimla and Shamsi. I was watching my miserable condition, my broken heart, and its impact on them. They understood my disgraceful condition, and so they avoided the subject and tried to divert my attention towards food, but my heart was agitated. I took their permission to leave and started alone. After walking a distance, my mind turned towards Shamshad Manzil.

I found Shama on the lawn. She was clad in a white dress, like the delectable Hourie of heaven. Her hands were full of jasmine flowers. As I went there, she showered those flowers on me smiling with excited anticipation and started joking as usual. Then she abruptly changed, intently looking at me. She started asking the reason behind my grief. How could I tell her that I had been deceived by someone for whom I was ignoring her? Instead, I was riddled with guilt. I asked her to give me a cup of tea as I pretended that I was not feeling well.

We sat in the corner, which was fully covered by the moonlight. Fortunately, I was also dressed in white. She said it looked as if two fish were swimming in the mercury river. I asked her not to be poetic then. Staying in the company of philosophers made you hate poetry. She was pointing in your direction. I was heartbroken and my heart was broken. When she intrigued, I told her not to taunt me for I was looking quite mardy, a typical lover. For God's sake I asked her to sing me a song instead, in a very canorous voice. Shama came near me and started singing a song about unrequited love. It gave me solace and sweetly reposed me. While singing, her voice turned raspier, and she started sobbing. She embraced me while sighing. I was nearing ecstatic satisfaction from all the excitement. When the heart paused throbbing, I started thinking about you again. You were so unlike Kaushaliya, Bimla, Shamsi, and Shama. Your inner and outer self were different. They were all one, from inside and out. Your high-rated philosophic thoughts' gild dazzled my eyes. They took out their hearts and put them before me, and I'm sorry to say I didn't value them. I was feeling shameful before Shama. This poor lady was moonstruck and silently worshipped me. Her craze for me was proverbial. She left the social gathering for my sake and kept herself aloof. She left colourful silk dresses and chose white, which is a symbol of her innocence and purity. She started learning to sing songs in dejection. I used to frequent her. Every time I went there, she would become an embodiment of affection and sing and, while singing, become sad. We used to visit a narrow hilltop and wander aimlessly on the deserted roads like insane people. As a result, I had to treat the injuries caused by your arrogance and hypocrisy. When it dawned, I would think of a new sun of reform that would rise in the sky of your life and bring changes in your life. Then I used to imagine the new thoughts for my future life, forgetting all about the past. However, after the night I witnessed in the club, I lost hope of any such miracle appearing. It was the final straw. I had dropped the idea of deceiving myself after the explosion. I called it a day and made our meetings formal and made my friendship virtual. I have decided to end this drama. Yet I didn't disclose this even before you. I gradually reduced my intimacy, open communication, severity, and devotion to you. That you received from me, you noticed this change and you enquired about this. But I was assured that there was nothing such. I met you, talked with you, dined with you, but I was all formal. As "Eat with a devil, but give him a long spoon,"

With the passing of time, the conditions changed. A massacre was caused, tumult appeared, the human race was scuppered, and the country was divided into two parts to make possible the impossible. Many beasts shared the responsibility of adding fuel to the fire. It seemed the waters of the Ganges and the Jamuna didn't flow as much as human blood flowed on the land of the Ganges and the Jamuna. Thousands of people become agitated. The concept and image of Delhi dissolved like anything. A new sun appeared in the sky with new hopes and new aspirations.

Though Delhi was down to the wire, the memories of Delhi didn't fade away. When situations become normal, I intend to shower flowers on the Taj Mahal of my memoirs. Ah! It was no longer the Delhi of Meer and Mirza Daagh. What could I do? Our fiction is all over the streets of Delhi. Loveable memories of the past are floating in the air. My stories can be found on every corner of the street.

Two years passed. Imagine how long this period of two years would be. Yet no one wants to describe it. What will happen? It looks as if centuries have passed, but it is taken easily. It looks as if they were not two years but two moments. Yes, even after this distance and indifference, I had information about every moment of your movements. I was always concerned about you.

At least you got information about my arrival in Delhi... and this morning you came to see me. What a warmth there was in your talk. How sparkling your eyes were! Your smile was very amusing. It looked as though you were coming after diving into the stream of loyalty. Don't you feel a risk of deflation now? I've become the same. A man of the same flesh and blood you wrapped your arms around my neck so tightly. What happened to your philosophy of flawless friendship? This is against the dignity of healthy friendship. Hasn't it lowered the dignity of friendship? It is deadly to one's reputation.

My life, you are very late! I am crunk now. Now I also opted for the way of the double life, like you. I am doubling down now in fact, now is very late! I am crunk now. Now I also opted for the way of the double life, like you. I am doubling down now. In fact, now you are qualified to love yourself. Come and kiss me. Then we will go for a cup of tea in this air.

After a while, we got up and went for tea. In the words of Rumi,

"In your light I learn how to love,

in your beauty how to make poems,

you dance inside my chest, where no one sees you,

But sometimes I do, and that sight becomes this art.

6-Bare Wounds

Iqbal Mateen

The concept of the arrival of first might be holding a bright prospect for someone else, for me it was a pain in the neck. It was a prelude to awaken all dormant plights: grocer, milkman, landlord, servant, scavenger, hairdresser, children's school fee, what and what not. The first used to arrive to my house as Dilnawaz, Vali Dakhni's the beloved used to come to his house secretly.

How to esteem the loyal beloved's arrival to my house

As the secret enters to my chest.

The first comes accompanied with turmoil and tumults, as conceived by Makhdoom: Take forward your life, take forward the world.

But the oncoming first stood before me like a mighty mountain of anguish. It was not less difficult than the expeditions of mountaineering of Ten Singh and Hillary. The Mount Everest was conquered by two but here I had to play a lone hand to meet the expenses of my house.

The conquerors of the Mount Everest the eager beavers at weel overcame the difficulties once and became immortal. But here the tension and toil unnerved body and periled the energy of mind and heart. If I could succeed in meeting the expenses of a month, there was none to applaud my maneuver.

There may be many more vanquishers of such ventures in this universe, who successfully exalt themselves by completing one expedition and prepare themselves to face the burden of the next. On the contrary the history pages on which their names are kept safe are commonly called office registers or epitaphs. They are not paid heed by any history student as either struggling movements are not included in the syllabus or removed from it.

In the wake of ceaselessly moved heaven and earth to reach the heights I stood fiddle-footed in the midst of frozen surroundings, vexatious, panting for breath, just then I found a Mr. Hillary. This Hillary, the endearing personality named Jitender. Jitender was one of the youngest officemates. He was not married so blithe, but he was at the threshold of the age where the woman's charm or exquisiteness, if doesn't arrest his attention, as merely a woman accentuates a microcosm. Jitender, breathing deeply in this universe, was ambitious to inhale deeply, the extract of the aromatic freshness of a woman, and transmigrate in himself, which could grasp the poison of the sinew of his youth.

To have access to the woman, the mountains didn't hinder in the way of Jitender that intervened us, my wife, my children, and me. The first of every month didn't fetch him the rarity that was the essential part of my fate. His deprivation was in fact different from me that was his ailing sister, who was elder to him. Her mother couldn't arrange to get from a florist, her floral wreath of bed, which would be decorated with raw buds and unbloomed flowers. The floral wreath of bed couldn't be arranged for her sister as she was ailing, and her body was inept of bearing the cold redolence of the flowers. Her breaths smell out the odour of medicines. To escape from it Jitender prepared his mind aromatic with the lurid fantastic charm of flights of fancy of a woman.

As per his statement, he was a scion, hailed from the affluent. He was affable and so showered a pledge on my wound making them wet with the balm of consolation. I open mindedly kept my glimmering wounds before his eyes however I found the beams of the sparkles of my wound breaking like rays. His eyes were not wet I felt he didn't address my miseries. He looked stolid. His face never wore sadness and reflected grief, on the contrary his face glittered. He buried his head in the sand.

I was chagrined; instead, he pricked my wounds with the emission of frenzied needles. The glittering freshness of his face gave my wounds a sore place, instead of giving me warmth. It was vexatious for me to think why his composure didn't change when I bend his ears about my little constrains and life's trivial events. Very soon he overcame his happiness, but the permanence of his complacency did not amend. I felt despite being a man from toff, he shouldn't ignore my pain like this.

'Don't worry?" He said keeping his hands on my shoulders.

"Woebegone situations don't lessen if we stop worrying?" I asked in a way that it's not me, but wounds got a tongue.

"Come to my house tomorrow morning, I will arrange money from a money lender on minimum rate of interest of rate."

"You will be sleeping like a bull then, unaware of the worries of the world." I said thus to fruitify the agreement.

"I wake up early in the morning." He said suppressing his joy.

"You seemed to be very happy." I asked him.

"Why I shouldn't be happy. I feel fortunate to help a friend like of you."

"Oh! Is this?" Really his helping nature impressed me, and I got relief.

"Yes, come well dressed, wear the suit you have." He suggested me "Okay broh! I will wear a suit, but where will you take me in good dressing?" "We have to impress that money lender." I laughed. He too laughed.

"Dear how many such fake dignified people will be wandering around him. However, brother, foppishness is stupendous and always palms off onlookers' ware."

I returned home with entire satisfaction. Jitender did full justice with his friendship otherwise in the age of 'each for himself', who tries to win others heart. Now victory over the Mount Everest was not an expedition. By tomorrow morning I would acquaint the Everest with the touch of my feet. I had no interest in whether I would get some reputation or not. Now I was not bothered, whether my wife and children would frequently utter my name or not. As soon as it dawned, I reached Jitender's house and stood on his door. When I knocked the door, an elderly woman opened the door and welcomed me. She took me inside respectfully and made me sit on the sofa and went I to inform.

I sat in the drawing room and started thinking about Jitender's riches. His words were echoing in my ears time and again. "Dear I inherited. Thousands of rupees, that are idly kept in the bank, but without my mother's permission I cannot draw even a single paisa. We can get everything in the world but not the mother. Mothers' happiness is a big blessing."

How sympathetic Jitender is! What an obedient son! What a responsible brother! I was wallowing these thoughts, suddenly a dignified elderly person entered in the drawing room. I got up from my seat to honour him. When I told him that I came for Jitender, he looked at me as I if I committed some mistake. When Jitender came there the first question I put about the elderly person. He said he was his uncle in relation. The matter dismissed there itself. We went on the expedition, when we neared the money lender's house; Jitender asked me, "do you want two hundred rupees?" "Yes, I said. "I already told you."

Jitender was moving with me quietly. When I asked him about reason his silence, he said he would introduce me to the money lender as his officer and I had to maintain the status of an officer. I laughed being mimetic... In order to make Jitender, I repeatedly mimicked our officer repeatedly he used to enjoy so much so that he used to burst in laughter, whereas now he was silent and smiled hardly.

While ascending the stairs of money lender's house Jitender said, "Dear you write a paper for two hundred. I also need one hundred, and I will pay the interest my amount." For the first time the secret the embodiment of Jitender's joy on seeing my wounds exposed before me. I understand now that the bits and pieces of my life didn't shake him. I felt as the zenith on the mountain on which we stood was much higher than that of the Mount Everest. I felt Ten Sing and Hillary were at the nadir. They were screaming from the intense bottom, 'you and Jitender are great. You have won an insurmountable task. You are immortal. The name of this cave is Everest.

I took the debt and formally I went to Jitender's house to leave him on the Rickshaw. When I reached his door, the voice of the elderly man was clearly heard whom I met in the morning. He was exclaiming, "Now your lad is also meeting his friends in the drawing room." The elderly woman, who opened the door for me was standing, was Jitender's mother.

The Blind Well

Awaz Sayeed
(March 1933–1955.)

The same blind, grim shadows were moving in the house today as usual, whereas he belighted the house bright in all rooms. Every time he felt as if these dark shadows would swallow him like a dragon and he would fall silently into a blind well. But his house was also a blind well, where he drowned and floated every day. It's a consternation that he felt as if someone was sneaking up on him and summoning him on his threshold. Who would summon him? There was no one who would address him by name, no friend or sympathizer. When his own children left him alone insouciant, with the excuse of a bright future, whom would he complain against? Is it not true that you are also selfish like my children?

No...no... all his friends were not like those whom he could subject to damnation and change the room, neglecting them when they come to meet him, and when ultimately, he grabbed, he would get enervated and flutter in eremophobia like an injured bird.

Then he saw a dead black crow and thousands of ugly crows stuck on walls were shouting. Why is this caterwaul? They could be playing bagpipes or complaining. It could be a protest. But how was he concerned with this complaint and protest? The clamour was mounting. It was a life-taking clamour. But what was it that they were carrying in their beaks?

Now there was death-like silence in his courtyard. It was a strange type of reticence, as if the air stopped suddenly while blowing. As if all the paths of the city were blocked. Who was standing stuck at the threshold?

No... No... Not at all...was It a superstition, but he was seen. His frozen lips were moving slowly as if he was passing through a test and anguish. But why was he standing there stuck to the threshold? Whether he was expecting the black, ugly crows to tuck him into their beaks and... Far... far away

No... No... That was one...

Did anyone make a call? Is he an earwitness to the call?

Call...?

The call ceilings were hit by a storm a long time ago. Now there were only ruins. Only ruins. A dreary graveyard... But in ruins, people roam about for water. Where are they? I feel ennui. I am tired of searching for them. Where are they? When my own children couldn't become an old man's staff for me, I was lorn...then these people.... No... No... In fact, these macho men were their sons. They are its children, or why would they come to these ruins?

What causes one to visit his house to look at him but the dismal calm creeps in this house of bright lights and gloom?

But how long would he be able to survive this claustrophobic suffocation? How long would a timorous man go without saying anything? Who prohibited him...Then why had he covered him with the sheet of silence? He was capable of tearing the counterpane of dumbness into pieces. But he doesn't want to expose himself before him. Any reason? No reason at all. He tried to stem the tide. If this is incorrect, then what is correct...Nothing is correct... everything is correct...But in between these two, there will be something, any path... any destination... The destination has no road. Not even the roads have a destination.

Did anyone contact me...

Nope... nope... nope...

Then where is this voice coming from?

Voice...?

Which voice... "Voice" has no name.

It might have some connection, at least.

Is it possible that he will die while standing on the threshold? But would he prefer to breathe his last in this desolate place? Is he a mistake? Isn't there any house... a top shed where he could go and...

But the source of this caterwaul, this clamour, and whether any dreadful black crow is dead in his courtyard are unknown. Then there was this caw... caw... raven sound... The frenzied screeches... The grains spread... the grain was pinched... What is this... everything...

Nothing!

This is merely a hallucination... A reverie... vorstellung... Is it whether one can dream while being awake?

Yes... it is possible...One can surely do it.

"In the middle of their dreams, yet they are awake in the dream," said one long ago...

I don't know anything... A Byzantine!

Then what is this suspense? ...what suspense...what veil...

One that's in between us...

But I'm lonely or my existence would be meaningless...in the middle of all the injured curtains of the house... Why are you befuddled? Why are all the roads closed?

The roads are closed for you, but not for me.

Straying might be the right sign of wisdom.

What do you mean by "might"?

You have the ability to recover yourself...

Mine?

Yes yours... Just before you tell us that all the curtains in your house are injured... Amidst your injured curtains, only you or your existence.

I agree with you. I didn't refute it.

Refusal implores before acceptance, or acceptance beseeches.

I don't want to entangle myself in the puzzle-ring of the words... You arrived here and unnecessarily bruised me.

For God's sake, get away from here. Why are you so timorous? That too, so soon. One who consumed the bitter poison of truth would be dauntless and would never be afraid of anyone.

But I notice you are afraid of me. I think you have tasted this poison for the first time. I sip it every day. On the contrary, I sip it like a soft drink, sometimes slowly and sometimes I gulp it quickly... very quickly.

Yet you are alive.

Aren't you noticing me? I am standing in front of you. Grope once... Look for me...If you don't put a bucket in the well, how will you drink water?

I am the parched, the well itself coming every day but my desire.... But it looks like you are also parched like me... from generations.

Have you come here to sneer at me?

Yes, every mask has an underlying reality... And every reality has a mask...

What do you want to convey? I gave you a forewarning... which I wanted to do... but now I'm blank... like you...

But what's this horrendous decimating sound? Caw, caw... Caw. Caw.

It is perilous! It sounds as if the ugly black crows of the world would ravage him... They take his pieces in their sharp beaks and carry him towards an unknown destination.

Zakath

WAJIDA TABASSUM

Years ago, on the occasion of Nawab Zain Yaar Jung's marriage, singing girls with tom-toms sang:

How crazy the people of this world are,

Why do they go on the roof?

Keep your eyes open and don't ogle,

The moon was shining on the earth, not in the sky Look at your courtyard and how the moon shines. He was really crazy. What would you call it if not a craze that he was staying in a mansion for so long a time, yet he didn't know that the moon shines not only in the sky but also on the earth? The festival was expected... People went on the roof to see the moon yesterday also... Neither Nawab's age was permissible nor was he happy fasting in Ramadan, for he had come with the permission of Allah to forego fasting and Namaz. In fact, the moon sighting gives pleasure to those who fast and complete Ramadan. Why did he prefer going up the roof? All the people insisted upon going up the roof, and the scholar of the mansion said, "The moon sighting on the sacred month's first would enhance vision, and it would also add to the good fortune." So, Nawab went up, not for the glory, but to improve his eyesight, which was deteriorating. He was reaching his forties, but right from the beginning he was a spendthrift of his youth. He was a philanderer. The destination of a stout sexagenarian was still far and not applicable. His previous life was eventful. He spent his infatuation so lavishly that his organs lost vigor. But he boasted that he was young. The clever and sharp-tongued widely experienced slave girls used to laugh, concealing their faces in the veil and disclosing nights' secrets spent with the Nawab and his inability to give orgasm.

"Waste! I don't know how last night passed. " "Waste! I don't know how last night passed. "

"Why? Did you get that much fondling?" The other would ask.

"Fondling?" She laughed and said, "I went and slept the whole night." He has flakiness, no strength in him."

"How are you moving with disheveled hair?" You didn't have a bath. I went to the bathroom. The hot water is as it is."

She felt uneasy and said, "If someone was unable to equip him and sleep, why should one have a bath?"

Despite all these whispers, Nawab Sab's youthfulness was unstigmated. After all, what was the use of the mansion's toady physician, who used to suggest to him that you should use budding wench more and more? If you do this, you will get more power.

Nawab went up the roof, not really with a bad intention. He went there to see the moon of the Eid. He couldn't see the moon. When people indicated to him to show the moon, he said, "Yes." And he fixed his eyes there. "

All of a sudden, his gaze slid from the end of the huge mansion and took a stand in the courtyard of the hut of a poor man. Though his vision was weak, and he couldn't witness the crescent. He examined the earthly moon with a fine-tooth comb. If a full moon was before, the poor eyes themselves would dazzle.

I was so insane; I'd been here for a long time and had never noticed such a blonde in my neighborhood.

His Deewan ji was ruing in front of him and wringing his hands.

"You didn't tell me that there was a doomsday in our neighbourhood." "Yes... Yes..." Deewan ji was embarrassed, "Yes my lord."

"I had not noticed."

"You need not notice. Do whatever it takes to get that girl before me. Do this much. "

He turned, opened the drawer of his cupboard nearby, took out a wallet with a tinkling sound, full of money, and tossed it toward Deewanji's feet and said, "We don't take anything free of cost. If that wench grumbles or the parents set a naught, hand them over this wallet." Even if they eat for their whole life, it doesn't end. "

The next day, Deewanji came there wringing his hands. He kept the wallet on the table and said, "My lord," but his tongue didn't cooperate with him express, "She..."

Don't bug me. What is this? She'...she'? "Speak quickly, whether something positive happened or not," Nawab said, losing patience.

"My lord, they are puritanical." The offer upset them. They said they would not sell their daughter. They are pious people. They arrange their daughter's marriage according to the religious doctrines sent by Allah and the Prophet Mohammed and bid their daughter farewell. They threw the wallet in my face."

Nawab gnashed his teeth with anger and said, "You human being! You should have told them to give their daughter in marriage." Deewanji trembled with fear. Nawab vents his spleen. He was not in the habit of using abusive words. He used to say, 'human being,' a good for nothing progeny. It was the worst abusive word for Deewanji.

"I told them my lord."

"What did they tell you that then?"

"They said you are advanced in age, and she is just tender aged."

When Nawabs heard the word 'tender aged", his blood boiled in his body. He asked, "Whether I look elderly?"

"No, my lord," Deewanji replied flatly, "you are still young, and many girls die..." couldn't complete his sentence. As he remembered the etiquettes, he bit his tongue.

Nawab burst into joy.

'That's what I was saying." Then he showed his avidity, but I should get the wench somehow."

"You are wise, my lord." Think it over. We are poor people with low wisdom. We will carry out your orders. "

"Try to enquire how many people stay in their family?"

"I have already enquired, my lord." Deewanji said immediately. A mother, a sick father, a bedridden grandmother, and three or four brothers and sisters. Ujala is the eldest of all. " Nawab's brain brightened on hearing the word 'Ujala.' "What a beautiful name!" he said, restlessly.

'The name is as beautiful as her face."

"Really, my lord, she is really brightness in the darkness." "Darkness becomes white when she appears."

"Now don't fawn on her too much." Nawab expressed his envy. "Go and tell the world that I am dismantling the entire street and making a new boundary." Ask them to vacate the street by this evening. "

"What a spiffing idea! Yes, my lord, very well. You thought intelligently. Where will they go with their big family? They have to surrender. "

"The parents of the girl appeared before Nawab, crying."

"My lord... sir..." We have spent our whole life on your feet. Where should we go now? Sick mother, who is unable to move she cannot stand, my man is a tuberculosis patient. We live under your tutelage."

"It would be nice if you shifted and enjoyed the facilities here in our servant quarters." We have much capacity. " "Nawab said softly, ingratiating her.

"My lord groked our difficulties." The mother lost her courage as she looked at her ailing husband. Confused, she nevertheless complied.

"I'm highly obliged to my lord." My lord, I say the truth; you are a great supporter of the subjects.'

It was a fact that Nawab Zain Yaar Jung was overgenerous. Hyderabad did not create a staunch head honcho than Nawab. He hated taking or accepting gifts from near and dear. His hands were always raised in giving. He had such hard faith in giving. He never lifted anything that fell from his hands on the ground. If anything fell on the ground, however precious it might be, he never bent. He used to make servants lift it and gift the item to them.

Generosity has been instilled in him since childhood. It was the first ever dose from his infancy. He never learnt to bend. Where did the Saudagar family, which has been dominating Hyderabad, get this wealth from? When a gold coin bag fell off his hands the Nawab called for his servant and asked him to lift the bag. When the servant tried to give him the bag, he spoke with a plum in his mouth, "You give us the fallen bag... You unreasonable nonsense, get out of here, take this bag and leave. "

His fate also favoured him with his bag. Later, it's said the parvenu established a business and he also led a life of Nawab's. Consider what he would be like as a child.

The Mansion' servant quarters were 'servant quarters' for name's sake. The ill-fated were fated to live luxuriantly, better than the lives of the affluent, but there was a doubt that always lurked in their hearts, not knowing what valuable the Nawab would claim for his beneficence. After all, what would Nawab ask? He believed in giving, not taking.

Buried under grace Sakina couldn't bear to sacrifice her life for Nawab. She was waiting in the wings. Somehow, she wanted to do something. She considers sending her children to press and massaging their legs.

Nawab smiled and said, "How can these small kids help?" If you want, send your eldest one. "

Whereupon her ears perked up, she looked at him. She remembered Nawab sending money to buy her daughter. As she did not sell for money now, he was asking to send her daughter behind the closed door. How could she do that? When she did not sell her daughter for money, how could she send her alone in the vacant room behind the door?

Nawab traced her facial expressions. "I know what you are thinking. But imagine if I wanted to kidnap her forcefully. Who could have dared to stop me?" Nawab persisted in his statement.

"Marry her, my lord. "Sakina said helplessly. "A young daughter's honour is like a glass plate, in a jerk it breaks."

"Marriage? Nawab said, perturbed, "Marriage means, responsibility for the whole life..." "heirs to fight for the property, are you crazy?"

Sakina asked in bewilderment, "My lord, your servant with a high cap came and said...she stopped as a measure of expediency."

Nawab said the truth. "I certainly said it, but my goal was to have ephemeral."

Ephi... ephemeral... She said stammering, "What's that, my lord?"

Nawab said frankly, "I went to my estate for weeks, so how can I stay without a woman? I married a wench and, while returning, I divorced her. Means a fixed time for marriage. Don't you worry if I divorce? I will give you a handsome dower so that your generation can comfortably live. When my thirst is satisfied...I can't say now, when I give divorce, but listen, I have done so many temporary marriages. But if a mean girl was expected to become pregnant to give birth to an heir, I would give her hot medicine and get her aborted. I don't want dirty bloody heir."

"No, my lord, illegal..." is unlawful.' Sakina was trembling from the core but was just at a loss for words. Her heart was in her mouth. She was not even capable of saying, yes or no, watching like a simpleton with her mouth agape open. Nawab was passed a verdict after the verdict. "I keep only one wife lawfully married." She is famous as Badi Pasha. I have learnt to give and give. I fix matrimony with them and then divorce them. After all, the poor also live from hand to mouth. If I don't give, what will happen to them? "

It felt difficult to go against the tide.

It was a dusty twilight evening when Nawab saw the moon shining from the roof.

Today he realized what light, 'Ujala', was!

God had blessed the poor Hyderabadi woman with an abundance of hair. Not only this... complexion, as if it was the moonlight flowing in the veins of the body, eyes... wine and treacle were worthless before it. Their eyes were designed to perplex and seize whoever she looked at. The height was, after all, In Arabic poetry, a woman's praise has been done thus: if a veil is put on a woman's body, it would hug the body at two places, one at the bust and the other on the posteriors; the rest of the veil would die to touch the body. Ujala had such a lavish body. She had such a bountiful embodiment that her veil would feel thirsty to hug the other parts of the build. The fair complexioned cheeks were decorated with killer cheeks that were the asset of Ujala. Nawab couldn't protect himself from the lips, which mostly wore a piercing sarcastic smile on them. Nawab was astounded by the fact that his strength had increased, and he no longer needed the assistance of a physician. He was revved up by the bod and body, which were full of diamonds, and pearls, gold and silver. He didn't see the need for marijuana electricity.

How ecstatic! Nawab was blessed with blissful moments! He satiated himself in such a way that the days being spent with Ujala looked to him as if they were heavenly. He had every pleasure, but Ujala didn't talk to him. He felt its necessity too, but his heart yearned for the double-stilled wine, the exquiteness, and this tribulation to spell out some charm from his mouth. But she used to bend her head with a piercing smile. With a simple nod, she would give her reply.

Although I have given you everything you required. But what if she had a desire?"

She used to give just a nod to express no.

Why are you so lyconic Ujala? You are so pretty. Your voice must be enticing. Speak something sometimes." She was so nonchalant that she gave a sneering smile.

He forgot his past; his past pleasures were a waste of time, juiceless, squandered.

She used to give just a nod to express no.

Nawab's sessions were grandiloquent, full of songs, music, and dance, as well as wine and women. He was a big-hearted Nawab. If any friend of his was inclined toward one of his temporary wives, he would immediately divorce her and present her to his friend. It was a simple example of his small generosity. Nawab's friends also took to the same trend. Nawab didn't accept any of the presents from his friends. He was born to give the answer. The question of taking from friends never arose. It was the same sense of seizure that night. Hot grilled minced meat was served in trays. Nimble aureate girls in transparent dresses were serving the wine. On the special orders of the Nawab, she was clothed in a golden guilded red dress. She entered the hall like a red-brimmed glass of wine. All were astonished, their breath stilled. Nawab sab was looking at the surroundings with pride. He blew his friends' socks off. She was twice intoxicated, one by the impact of wine, the other by the feeling of ownership of such a unique and ravishing belle that had no second. He was gradually regaining consciousness in order to respond.

"This is called a raving beauty." Someone said being berserk "And this is known as gait. This is the delectable hourie of heaven we heard of, but we see it first. "

"What will Nawab sab get after death?" Here he is taking pleasure in heaven. " "But how much did this valuable diamond cost you?" Nawab sab looked around with pride. Not known what he was going to say...

For the first time in his life he spent with Ujala, the mellifluous flute touched his ears out of nowhere... "Who was asking the Nawab sab this question?" She defiantly asked him. Further, she said, "You know, Nawab Zain Yaar Jung is a very big Nawab, big hearted, very generous, only gives doesn't take." But this poor wench from Hyderabad, from a small hut, is not less generous. I will tell you that the Nawab, who doesn't accept anything from others, has taken my alms. I gave him my beauty in charity. The first in the line of beggars was he who was standing before me, spreading his chattel. I have heard he has not accepted any presents from anyone but only given them. But I ask you why, as he accepted the alms of my beauty. "What is his status to me? I myself have made him a beggar."

Nawab, who was always desirous of hearing her voice, Today, after he heard, he was embarrassed. He felt as if someone had poured melted metal into his ears. He couldn't hear anything further. The glass of wine fell from his hands. He too waved and came down to the earth, never to rise again.

In Search of Heaven

Jeelani Bano

"Assalaamualaikum sir."

All the students became happy when they saw the teacher.

"Sir, I will write a letter to Allah asking Allah to grant our father a large sum of money." Munni said happily.

"No, my kid, we cannot write a letter to Allah." The teacher tried to explain it to the child.

"Why?" Doesn't Allah know Urdu? " Munni asked in wonder.

The teacher collects the orphans, guttersnipes, poverty-stricken children, and labourers' children to educate them on the teachings of religion.

"Pray to God. He will accept your prayers. "The teacher said to them.

"Baba... I am blind... Give me one rupee. Allah will give you a thousand. "An old beggar was asking for alms while standing at the door of the mosque.

"Will Allah accept his prayers?" one of the children asked the teacher. "Then why doesn't he ask for one thousand from Allah?" The child asked.

"Stop this useless talk..." "What did I say yesterday?" the teacher asked.

Don't tell a lie... and don't steal. "Perform namaz."

"Sir... Munni tells a lie... One of them pushed Munni forward a bit...

"She stole sweets from a shop."

"So... Was Allah watching me?" Munni asked in worry.

"Yes, keep your nose clean. Allah watches everything. " Every act is done at His wish. "

"Oh! Shakir, who was sitting near Munni, said.

"How does Allah do so many things?"

My homework is not done after coming from school. I told the teacher a lie that I was suffering from a fever. Shakir addressed his friends who were sitting near him.

All the children started laughing. But the teacher chided them. "Silence..."Mannerless kids... "

"If you tell a lie and commit theft, Allah will put you in hell." The teacher hid his face in horror and looked at the children.

All the children were frightened. Munni and Shakir looked sideways, petrified.

"What happens in the hell..."Another girl asked.

"Hell is a very dreadful place." The teacher made his face terrified and said that the children might be afraid of it.

"Those who do evil deeds commit theft." Tell a lie and you will be put in hell. "The teacher said

"Where is the hell, sir?" One of the boys asked, "Being scared stiff?"

Hell is in the sky... It will be totally dark there. We will not get food if we feel hungry. There is no water to drink... Scorpions and snakes will be biting ever. Neither do we get bedding, not even a blanket to cover ourselves. " The teacher made his face fearful to tell them about the punishment of hell. All the children came near and listened attentively to the teachers' talk with concentration. They looked towards the sky to see the hell there.

"I will not go to hell." A young girl, whose heart was in her mouth, said, hiding behind Munni... But Munni held her hand and said to Razia, "Don't worry." Why are you afraid? The teacher doesn't know if hell is not in the sky... " Munni held Razia.

"Oh! Tommyrot! Am I speaking falsely... "The teacher got angry and spoke.

Then... what's the hell do you know? "The teacher asked Munni.

"Yes, I know," Munni said, protecting herself from the teacher's cane.

"You come with me..." I will take you to hell. "

"What nonsense are you talking about?"

The teacher raised his cane in anger.

"Piffle...you make fun of me." "You will take me to hell." The teacher said,

When Munni saw a cane in the teacher's hands, she was alarmed. She hid herself behind her companion, kept her hands on her ears and started crying.

"I am not telling a lie." There's nothing wrong with calling a spade a spade Sir." Our hut is in hell in our village. When my father comes home, rat-arsed, he beats my mother. Then my mother says, "Crying, this house is not a house but a hell." She expressed an empirical theory, as what she heard from the teacher looked outlandish.

"I see..." Your mother says, "Your house is a hell." The teacher asked.

"Yes sir, our house is also hell... You say that there will be no light in hell... No food to eat, no water to drink... We don't have a lamp. When oil dries, it becomes dark... We don't have food to eat or water to drink. A child said.

"And we have to carry water from so far, and in the night no water will be there to drink." Another child said.

"Our father doesn't get rice in the night, so our mother puts stones in the pot to pretend she is cooking." A child said and started crying. Our grandmother doesn't come here, that's why... She says, "We have the sky as a roof to cover and ground to sleep on." We all started laughing.

"And if it rains, it comes into our house."

"A snake came into our house last night."

The teacher hung his head in shame when he heard them. Whatever the children said was fair and square.

Now what percept can be given down the road? What torment should I talk about to scare the children to prevent them from evil deeds.

Suddenly, some shrieks were coming from outside the mosque. People started shouting and crying.

He could hear the sound of fire. People were running helter skelter. Traffic was cordoned off.

A bomb was blasted at a splendid hotel.

The place of the labourers caught fire. Huge flames were seen everywhere. The children started crying due to panic.

The teacher also wanted to get rid of the children to take shelter somewhere.

All the children came up to the teacher and embraced him.

"How can we reach home?" "Sir, we are scared."

"Sir, why did hell come down to earth today?"

"Sir, why are you carrying us towards hell?" Let's go towards heaven. "

The teacher was worried about the children's questions, so he took the children in his hands and stood in a corner trembling with panic.

"Oh Allah, you have sent hell on earth for these children."

Why do you postpone your plan to enter heaven until the end of time?

Show me the way to take these kids to heaven.

King Makers

M M Mahshar

My fleet-footed car was on the highway. I don't like high speeds, and on every occasion, I preferred evenness. I didn't know that the speed was looking good. My driver was an accomplished one. I had entire faith in his skill. It was my forefathers' village on this road, which was left thirty years back. None of my relatives live there now. Many reminiscences of my childhood started knocking at the door of my heart. The aroma of freshly moistened swings; picnics in the fields during the rainy season; the bank of the stream, the cool breeze, sand houses, the spring of the holy Ramadan; the grief of Muharram commemoration, thick large loaves, the flavour of date like fried wheat lumps, sweet pies filled with grated coconut mixed with sugar, and the earthen pots filled with rice pudding, the fatiha (recitation of prayer on the eleventh of the month), offering on this day for the Sunnite saint Abdul Khader Jeelani, peace be upon his soul, the rituals of marriages, what to remember and what to forget. I was as keen as mustard to see my village.

As the village was nearing, my heartbeat became fast. My heartbeat was keeping pace with the car.

I asked my driver, "A village will come in some time." I want to see that. We will stop there for a while. "

He was slowing down his speed. After some time, our car entered the village. The mud road, on both sides of which there were tamarind trees, about which there were many rumours, had disappeared. The broad tar road announced the progress of the form. The Darshan trees with red flowers presented the image of a newlywed bride covered with the red corner of a mantle drawn over her face. The outmoded tales of the darkness were announced by the electric poles on the roadside.

My car entered the village. In the centre of the village there was a round building which was called 'Gol Chowdi," meaning "the junction of four roads." In fact, it was a bus bay, where one bus used to come every day, and many people hung around waiting for the bus to come. There were several small and large shops surrounding this 'Gol Chowdi,' which resembled a nimbus around the moon. Among all these, there was Mullah saith's big cloth shop. It was always filled with customers. Many salesmen used to work there. On the occasion of festivals and marriages, the customers had to wait for their turn. The original name of Mullah saith was not known. He was the leader of the mosque without any remuneration. He taught children the holy Quran, the commemoration and rehearsal of prayers, the recitation of eulogies, hymns, corpse-laving, and chicken and sheep slaughtering. Many families benefited from being fed by the alms, which amounted to 2.5 percent of their income. No beggar used to go empty-handed from his shop. That was the reason he was called Mullah saith. There was a cobbler just beside Mulla Saith's shop. There was a stall of a cobbler whose voice was voluminous, so he was called Ponga Cobbler. Besides this, there were the shops of a tailor, a washer man, and a hairdresser. A woman, Lachamma, used to fry basin-covered chilies, the aroma of which spread throughout the whole bazaar. The 'GolChowdi' has now changed into a big four-way crossroad. "The Gol Chowdi' was changed into a small garden where a statue of a leader was mounted. In the place of Mullah saith there was a big show room. Moorthy's shop was changed into a supermarket known as "Moorthy and Sons." When I went there to ask about Mullah Said, I just clammed up after I knew about him.

Behind the counter, I found the picture hanging which was garlanded. I tried to recognise the man who was sitting on the counter. My doubt changed into reality. It was Ramesh, the elder son of Ponga Cobbler.

"Whose photo is this?" I asked him, indicating the Ponga cobbler's photo with my finger.

He gazed at me, turned towards the photo, and said, "He is my father."

"Oh! So, you are Ramesh? " I asked.

"Yep, I am Ramesh." He had wonder in his eyes.

"Where are your brothers Umesh and Naresh?'

"They are in the USA. Long ago, they left. They are engineers in a firm there."

"Hmm!" I could not say anything further and started looking towards the road. It was blustery, and the polythene bags were flying higher.

"Here there was Mullah saith's shop," I asked, being a little embarrassed.

"Yes... yes." He is no more. We bought this from his sons. "

"Where are his sons, Hashim, Kazim, and Nazim now?"

"Look there at that corner. His elder son, who is fixing the puncture of a vehicle, is Hashim. "I turned towards him. The winds slowed down. The polythene bags were coming down the stairs. I accelerated towards him without asking any other questions. When I reached there, I saw a lean man, aged forty, in untidy clothes, who was rubbing the tube with sandpaper. I greeted him.

He raised his head and looked at me attentively. He spat his gutkha and said, "Walaikumassalaam." I had a face like a wet weekend. It was sad that the next generation of Mullah saith didn't brace itself with an air of tomorrow's undertaking. It didn't burnish itself, or perhaps it was left to its devices.

"Are you Hashim?" he asked recklessly. When I enquired about his brothers and sisters, he said, "Look! Kazim, runs a tea stall, Nazim runs an auto, and the third one used to sell cinema tickets in black. He is in jail. Sadiqua's widow works in Moorthy's shop, cleaning groceries. Jameela's husband divorced her, so she is cleaning utensils and mops in Ponga Cobblers' house. "Good grief!" I shuddered. Mulla Saith was an esteemed personality, highly respected by one and all. People used to salute him while standing from their seats when he moved through the streets. I heard about the disastrous position of his family. Mullah Seth weighed in on a plan and his sons couldn't. It troubled me a lot. I tried recreating myself with the remembrance of romantic thought; a stream in the village, flowing in between hills, presents the picture of a bride whose line of parted hair is radiant with glitter powder. This stream flows out of the village; sand-made houses, young girls being coquettish near the quay, young boys swimming far on bets, and the fishermen spreading net to catch fish. I sat in the car and asked the driver to drive out of the village.

This village comprised five hundred and sixty houses, of which about twenty-five houses belonged to the Muslim community. Most of the people belonged to weavers' families, Velmas (a sub caste in the Hindu community) and the Reddy community. The rich had Bengaluru tile houses, and middle-class families had ordinary tile houses. The Schedule Caste people had grass huts.

Now there is a sea change. Only RCC buildings were lined up. When the village ended, we searched for the stream. We became happy when we saw the stream. There was a huge and splendid temple built on the bank of the stream, where the chants and bells were echoed. The stream shrank like an old woman of eighty. Water was slowly moving the burden of flowers and leaves. There was no quay, no youthful girls. In the place of sand-made houses, there were ditches from where sand was trenched and carried away for RCC construction. I did not like this misty atmosphere.

I was returning. It was time for evening prayers. I thought of performing namaz in our old mosque. I asked a Muslim boy about the location of the mosque. He indicated the next lane and laughed meaningfully. I couldn't understand the reason behind his laughter.

My car stopped in front of the old mosque. It was decayed. Its doors were eaten by termites. It was surrounded by wild bushes. Its desolation or depopulation was worse than that of Cordoba, an Islamic state ruled by the Umayyad dynasty. It was not destroyed by strangers' hands.

I recollected the mosque of the Mulla saith period: thickly populated, eventful life, the splendour of Ramadan; the sittings on the celebration of Prophet Mohammed's birthday. I found a bearded old man and questioned him, "Uncle, don't Muslims reside here?"

"Yes, of course, about forty houses."

"Then why is this mosque deserted?"

"My son," he pulled no punches," this is a dereliction of duty. All people idly wander here and there. They go out in the morning and come home late in the night, tired, eat, drink, and sleep. "Who cares about Namaz and observing fast?" the old man replied excitedly.

My mind stopped thinking as I was just at a loss for words. I came to my car, and it sped up towards the town.

It was an election moment. Meetings were conducted everywhere. A leader under the saffron-coloured flag was gushing about, "These insignificant insects, which cares about them? They can be crushed at any time like ants; it doesn't make a difference if they vote for us or not."

I proceeded and found a green-colored camp from where a bearded man was shouting at the top of his lungs, "Don't forget we are king makers." We hand over government to whom we want and snatch it whenever we want."

Some bunkum was going on there.

What a piffle! Who can hold a mirror up to these firebrands who loyally and steadily work for their lords?

I was thinking which box is most befitting for people who cannot stand the test of time and have failed to be a bellwether.

Bonfire

Qamar Jamali

"Bosh...um..."

The leper threw the last piece of firewood into the bonfire, uttered, and joined his lips firmly together.

Now the scarlet flames were dancing, and the leper looked very much pleased. When the wind blew hard, the flames grew more scarlet, and the leper's eyes enlivened a familiar spark.

Scarlet red...

Reddish fire of man's stature...

Rejoicing reddishness in his eyes...

The reddishness of his wife's hem...

When the flames in the bonfire rose, he felt redness everywhere...

It happens the same way in the experiments of aesthetics. In visibility, vision disappears and remains only a scene...

"Arrived..."

He burst with joy. He made an unsuccessful attempt to stand but fell again on his hands. His throat lets diverse sounds in mirth...

Then he became rapturous...

He raised his stump of arm in the air and dances haphazardly...

Meaningless...dance...

Sour- faced...round red eyes out of eye-sockets. Two thin nasal mucosae on the face in the name of nose... stump of arm...when he rose them, he looked not a human being but a cobra...that dances frenzily the light of cobra pearl.

"AAnchana...My bride...

When flames became dim, he enflamed them and spread his arms and made an effort to embrace them.

"Come...make a way into me...or else...lug me in you.

The leper knew the destination of his love. His ruined body apparently didn't go with his emotions. But he was not to be blamed for this.

He was not a leper by birth.

His brain was as young and unsullied as it was thirty years back. No idea how he came under the influence of an evil eye in his exuberant youth.

He was full of life.

Rapturous limbs.

It was difficult to live with lurgy, with this ruined, afflicted, decaying body among the people with a whole body. He only knew. How difficult it was to live with this perceived living death was evident. He only knew how he lived thirty years of this horrible, transgressive life. He was worn out severely from dancing quite madly, being completely unnerved and beginning to sweat.

He felt blue. He hates himself...he loathed his existence...his stinking rotten flesh, and the stench of decomposing flesh.

He wishes to die.

Death...

How would be his death...? His relation broke off with his mirror long back.

"No... They are not ordinary wounds...leprosy... it can cause deformities of hands and feet. It can affect organs. It can affect the nerves, skin, eyes and lining of nose. If it was not treated in time and spread and the bones would melt like wax..." The doctor unsparingly declared.

The last time...

Yes, that day he looked into the mirror the last time. he suddenly started noticing his nasal bone collapsed like a roof without foundation... he was watching...watching...he saw his face becoming dreadful. In place of nose there were only two holes.

He was hissing in resentment.

And...

The mirror cracked. His brain was filled with doom and gloom. The pieces of his face were scattered seen in the shards. Every organ was broken into pieces. He had no guts to see the figure of the pieces. not even any ambition provoked him to see his image.

And...

That day...

He saw his bride drew close in the red hem, pulling it to her feet for the last time

Yes...

On that day...

He saw...red flame gleaming on her wife's white cheeks. He felt as if the flames of fire rising from her face. He was horrified and overturned the hem of her dress in panic.

The colour of a bright flame was scattered.

His eyes consumed the redness.

He was trying to grope his wife like a blind. A terrible shriek came out of his throat. He felt, he gulped the whole bonfire.

Nothing remained but... Only the glow remained... being a sight.

When he saw the distance between the two beds in his bedroom, he was sure that life was extracting a ransom, gradually in installments.

Then...

The distance was widening.

There remained only one cot in the room.

His relationship with his wife was to the extent of talk...

She was decreasing like the moon. In the name of a married woman only red vermillion remained in the part of the hair. His infant was sent to orphanage.

And...

One day...

The carpet of his wife which was exactly Infront of his room was also removed.

Then...

Fourwheel...a hand cart.

Home...

Hand cart...

Home...Cart...home...

Bash...Um...

He grew uncontrollably sad and took the silver pot in a huff and threw it on the fire...some sparks erupted instantaneously.

"Scream?... you treacherous fellow!... You would be extinguished in a short while...Or...

A gush of wind came and carried away the sparks far. He screamed at the top of his lungs increasingly uncomfortable.

"Look...what I said...He would come...Your paramour...you lover...You would elope with it...

A stormy air blew intermittently. The sparks in the ash enlivened again for a moment...red sparks appeared in the white ashes...and took wing...

As I expected...wait...where do you shift cruel fellow...

He took the footwear, wore in his stump of arms started running fast stamping his hands on the ground. He was aghosted. The puff of wind was his rival that always raised and enticed the hidden sparks.

"I will kill you...Do you hear me?"

"Who...who do you Baba?"

He didn't notice he came towards the populated areas from dreary lonely fields. He stopped and saw the surrounding.

"Yes...who...who would he kill?" how could he reply to it?

There was no one there.

He was absolutely exhausted with the urging of the vigorous man inside. It was defeated again and again by the ruined body. He tried thousands of times, but it made him livelier. He was sometimes angry with his passions and sometimes loved them.

The connection between the brain and the body was incomprehensible.

They repulsed as he tried to press them. That day he desperately remembered the one with whom he learnt the first lesson of life. He knew it was quite natural.

But...

But...but...but...why again but appeared?

This word...it's not a word it's a sign of defenselessness.

This is the word that draped his life like a spider's web. He hated it. Yet it stands before him like a milestone at every step and extended the term of his vulnerability.

He wanted to cry...

But...

No, he wanted to laugh, as he wanted life.

Probably...He wanted to seize her in his arms...Behind the scarlet veil...He wanted to chug down many goblets of wine with the big astonishing open eyes.

She was the well of sweet water.

But...

But he remained above... like a broken bucket.

And rope...?

The infectious disease gnawed him.

Just one end of it, which instead of cutting and diminishing, upturned in him. It was the same end of the rope that was causing tumult in him.

I want to live...with you...are you hearing me...? Under the coolness of your hem...

Look how frightful I am looking...but..."

Again, the same but...the spider-web, in which he was writhing like an insipid ant...

I want to liberate myself from this evil spirit...I want to live with you instead, in the four walls...that is home...

"Baba...hope you also had a home?"

In order to free himself from the cobweb, he lied on the ground face downward, turning left and right, it jostled him again.

"Home...?" He looked four ways.

"Hope you had a home before?"

"Home...at home...Yes, I want to stay alive...being at home...

"With whole body like of you..."

There was no one...He was all alone...his broken existence...which was breaking steadily, muscles ...and veins deteriorating from inside and outside.

Now he was running backward...with utmost speed...toward his shelter...where he established his world.... the pile of grass and straws...broken footwear and useless plastic plates...He was running...

He was running with incredible speed, on four wheels and...on his two hands.

The winds cleaned the place where he lit bonfire. The wind carried away even ashes.

Only a feeling remained...a sign of life...sense of human life... a white dot which thrived... a dot...straw...grass...broken footwear useless broken plates.

Now dance will take place here...the dance of red flames...She would come...Anchana... Voluptuous body...scarlet hem...my schatzi...

I will dance...with you...under the shade of your hem...I need you...I require your warmth...after all you are my need...

You are my better half... it's written in Upanishads.

He was shouting from the depth of his lungs...He was panic stricken...

"Bash...um."

The leper took out a match box from his chattel and threw the burning fire stick in the pile of garbage.

Fire started bouncing... he was mirthful...His body began to heat up...sparks were blowing up...

The leper was frenzied...His round red eyes widened and became frightful...He tried to get up from the coach but failed. He squated on the coach helplessly.

A gush of air passed.

Countless spiders were creeping on his body...

The leper grew apprehensive...

No...It would not happen today...You cannot quit me like this...at least you can't elope with your paramour...

Because...

I want to amalgamate in your existence...amalgamate in you...

After all you are my requirement...

Bash...um."

The leper waved his hands in the air like an astroaught...

And...

The stench of burning flesh spread in the air.

Tower Of Silence (Dakhma)

Professor Baig Ehsas

Sohrab's bier (corpse) was ahead of us. It was followed by two white clad Karters (Zoroastrian

Priests). Walking serenely, they arranged themselves into a pair of two, each holding a pay wand. We were following them and stopped at the gate. At the gate, we stopped as we were non-members.

We were forbidden from entering the gate.

I explored the vicinity. Everything was the same. Things were as they had been. Nothing changed at my sister's house. I had no one here in this house. My elder sister and brother-in-law were dead. My niece was staying here in this city with her husband.

I used to come to my sister's house to spend vacations. She was the eldest sister. I had six sisters.

I had three sisters in between her and I, and I was the youngest of all. I was their only brother. My niece was two years younger than me. We used to play together more. I was fond of this house. It was a splendid house built on the rock beyond the railway station.

The buildings were made with great planning. A straight tarmac road passed in between the buildings. The road had up and down. A road wagon was used to ply the roads of this twin city.

The entry of rickshaw pullers and cyclists was restricted. By the time the buggy reached my sister's house, the horse would be out of breath. The horse would move at a moderate rate, and the man had to balance in a particular way when we got down from the buggy. There was a reservoir.

The house and St. Philomena's church were on the house's east side, where the road was even. There was a missionary school in the church, where Muslim girls rarely study due to the skirt uniform. My niece was studying at Islamia School. We have seen every nook and corner of the church, as children were not stopped from entering. The Christians of the area used to gather in the church. On Sundays. It pleased us when the church would ring. I'm not sure who used to call them.

The mosque was a distance from the colony, where there were small uneven houses.

There was a round building on the rock in front of our house. It was an area spread over many acres of land. It had a huge boundary. Below it, there was a big gate. It was called "PADRI.GUTTA"

A small house was built in the surrounding area, where a watchman, his wife, and a dog stayed, a mysterious dog. In many houses, there were Alsatian dogs. This dog was different from others. From afar, it looked as if he had four eyes.

She used to say children should not go there. Moving in a row, holding one corner of the handkerchief each. Two priests on the front, a vehicle in between, a row of parsis behind, turned. A wake of vultures started appearing. They all sat on the corner of the circle-like building. They flew by evening. I have never seen such a kettle of vultures before. They were all busy till the evening. I asked my sister, why did such a volt of vultures gather on the circle-shaped building? My sister informed me that it is a Parsi graveyard and that Parsis leave dead bodies on the roof for the vultures to consume. All the vultures came for that purpose.

"What type of ritual is this, AAPI?

"Each religion has its own beliefs. Some people buy, some people cremate, and when Parsis bodies are devoured by vultures for excarnation, they take it as virtuous. The vultures return before it is night. Despite their return, we didn't sleep that night on the roof of our house. My niece and I slept in the house because of fear that we might be eaten by the vultures, which take us to be dead.

After waking up, we went to the Parsi Gutta. The dog started barking when he saw us. He asked,

"You, my children?"

"Uncle, did anyone die yesterday?"

"Yes, son."

"Why do two people move in a row?"

"This is the procedure. Nobody moves alone."

Why did they hold a hanky? "

"This is not a hanky, this is a paywand."

"And what about this round structure?"

"This is Dakhma. Its roof is high in the middle, with three circles on the ceiling. A male dead body is kept in the outer circle, a woman's in the middle, and a child's in the inner circle. They are kept open to be baked by the sun, and they can be seen by the vultures. The dead are placed here so that they are open to the elements as well as birds of prey."

"Why is this dog strange?"

"This is Sagdid. It didn't have four eyes." The four-eyed dog is meant to be a dog with two eyes-like spots just above the two eyes. This Sagdid determines whether a man is virtuous or a sinner. "

"How uncle?"

"When you grow up, you will understand it," he answered, weary of the queries.

"And uncle, where do these vultures come from?" "If sugar falls on the floor, where do the ants?"

What caused it to appear?" The watchman put this question and went in. (Sohrab was also passing through all these procedures.)

Sohrab's tavern was in the busiest part of the town. It was possible when his ancestors opened that it might not have been that busy, as the Raja Sahab mansion was just in front of this wine shop. There was also a big mansion beside this. To its right was a drama theatre, and to its left was the Britishers' residency. There was a mosque before it. A lane beside the mosque went to the bachelors' house. "Mujarrad Gah" is the meeting place for writers and artists. It had a fine arts academy and an office for a magazine. We used to go there to see the writers. In those days, some poets were no less famous than film actors. There was a wine shop in front of the bachelors' house where cheap liquor was available. Most of the artists used to go there. When they earned something, they frequently went there. This is the oldest wine shop. Sohrab used to sell pure wine, and he was well acquainted with the nature of writers. He used to admire the good verses of the poets. Parsis are usually good-mannered and cultured. He used to charge only the cost of wine, water, and glasses he used to supply. There were tables and chairs inside. Crisps and snacks were not arranged there. Children used to carry roasted green peas, groundnuts, and poha. Customers used to purchase items from them whenever needed. It was a cheaper bar when compared to those of others. When we started to go to the tavern 'Maikada,' the city had passed through many changes. The communist movement against the sovereign, the Telangana Movement, was successful, but the kingship was put to an end by the new government of Congress. Police action has horrified the Muslim community. They were out of their senses. There was a great revulsion in the public. Hardly had nationals recovered from the division of the country in the name of religion when further divisions on the basis of language established further limitations on boundaries. The state was broken into three parts. This was like an attempt to beat a dead horse. Years have passed, but the divided parts, which were larger than the states into which they were merged, are still unable to become one. It was like oil and water, incompatibility due to fundamental differences in personality and opinions. Due to the inflexibility of basic cultures, these parts of the state present the look of a graft of sack cloth in velvet. The partition of the country was unacceptable to the nation and the division of the state on the basis of language and its limitations were not accepted by the owners of one language people. Two different cultures!

The city, which has no history and no culture, got the upper hand. The stable power had fallen into their hands as a result of political force. They frantically occupied the vacant land. On the one hand, big mansions were made into portions and sold. It was against the tradition of the place to dispose of land, so out of shame; the land was sold at dirt-cheap rates. The intruders purchased lands and became millionaires. New localities were fully developed.

A big mansion was changed into a head post office; an engineering office was shifted into a mansion, and another mansion was occupied by the AG's office; a big hotel was opened in a different mansion. The gardens were taken away by the Bazars, and the government took away Lady Hyderi's club.

The palace of King Koti was occupied by the government hospital; the jail building was dismantled and turned into a hospital. A big mall was opened in the theatre, built on a Roman pattern. A commonplace, frivolous city was rising in the unique city of gardens, mansions, lakes, and concrete roads. Everything changed in a few days. Some of the representatives of culture who could protect it either crossed the border or settled in western countries. The heir-apparent settled in the west. The patriots who ever returned to the state felt as ecstatic as when the conqueror returned to his throne.

Neither the royal class nor the affluent people, nor the common masses, are annoyed at the loss of culture. A government hospital was built in the vicinity of the tavern.

A government hospital was established in Rajaji's mansion. In the front mansion, the main office bank shifted. The residency was changed to a women's college, and the drama theatre was changed to a cinema theatre. The city map was fast changing. The Telugu film industry shifted here from Madras. The splendour of the town was on the rise. There are film studios, 70-millimeter movie theaters, and massive shopping malls. Cloth shops, gold shops, all belong to them. The hotels were established in accordance with their food habits, where a man of average income could take full meals. When they mix curd into their rice and eat it, the liquid of the curd falls from their hands to their elbows. The strength of girls and boys with brownish complexions was increasing. Large black kajal eyes, salty expressions, and the broad back-neck of the blouses. I'm not sure why these people enjoy exposing their backsides.

The locals were compelled to purchase the dry tank land from the land grabber and construct their houses on it. Every rainy season has been proven to be doomsday. Communal riots affected the status of the old city, and a curfew was prolonged for weeks together. Curfews lasted for weeks. Every festival was celebrated under the shadow of fear. Due to the prevailing conditions, many families relocated from the old city to the new city. All the charm, broad roads, flyovers, and high-tech cities were in the new city. Only a few historical buildings remain in the old city.

During the festival, the market was open and shining all night. Two different cultures couldn't coexist, so they made separate islands. When the locals felt deprived, they demanded a separate state, and the firebrand took advantage of this by inflaming the debate during the election. There used to be a hustle and bustle. The area around the 'Maikada' was turning into downtown. I was one of the members who shifted from the old to the new city.

There is no meeting point for writers and poets these days. All became helter-skelter. It could be considered a period of confusion. A man was taken by a machine, and loneliness was accepted as our fate. It was accepted that the traditions of historical, cultural, national, social-emotional, and religious harmony were destroyed. The whole of literature was in the grip of caste consciousness. So, it was unnecessary to sit together in the hotels or bars. The city expanded. We gathered in a friend's house, or wine was brought from any nearby shop. Refreshments could be ordered on the phone, as the home delivery trend began. The concept of "Maikada" was out of fashion. The area of Maikada was turning into the downtown. I was one of the members who shifted from the old to the new city.

(People were still busy in Dakhma; nobody came out yet.)

There is no meeting point for writers and poets these days. All became helter-skelter. It could be considered a period of confusion. Man was taken by a machine, and loneliness was accepted as our fate. It was accepted that the traditions of historical, cultural, national, social-emotional, and religious harmony were destroyed. The whole literature was in the grip of caste consciousness.

So, it was unnecessary to sit together in the hotels or bars. The city was widened. The city expanded. We gathered in a friend's house, or wine was brought from any nearby shop. Refreshments could be ordered on the phone, as the home delivery trend began. No concept of "Maikada."

'Maikada' was out of fashion.

Why was he thinking about the city? Was it because the closure of 'Maikada' surprised him?

Part of the culture was dead. My friend Musheer, who went to the USA with a dream of a better life, came back to India after 20 years.

Those who leave their country either grow nostalgic or become anxious to do charity work. He wanted to visit every place where we had gone in the past. He moved in with me and used to get sad about the changes. Yes, the city has changed rapidly. The glimpses of globalization were clearly noticeable. He bemoaned what he saw in the USA as a sign of progress being imitated here. The city was losing its identity, and all were becoming alike. I remembered only one thing that remained unchanged, and that was the tavern, which faced no change: the same building, the same arrangement, the same counter, and continuity of customers. The people who bought bottles took them as a requirement and used them to save the remainder. The next day, they were surprised to find not a single drop had been reduced.

Honesty was the specialty of the tavern. Most of the customers felt a great kinship here. We used to come every day until Musheer departed, sit up to a specific house, and then return. I didn't know Musheer didn't recall 'Maikada.' After he was back from the USA, he didn't even take the name of liquor. I told him I would take him to the place where he stayed the same. The next day I took him to the 'Maikada.'

The Maikada was closed. EST.1904 was embossed on the forehead of Maikada. Years back. When I inquired about it in the neighborhood, I discovered that it had been closed for along time. I was shocked. I felt sorry for my ignorance. I didn't know how it happened. I felt apart of the culture had died. I didn't know how Sohrab was. Does his business have a jerk? Was he trapped in some foudroyant situation?

We asked about his address, reached there. It was a Parsi-fashioned building. The servant escorted us to the drawing room. We sat there and started watching the frames hanging on the walls. Sohrab didn't make us wait there.

"You!" he exclaimed, looking at me.

"Yes, did you recognise him?" "Musheer." "Oh yes, I called to mind. You look quite a white man."

"An American." I said and laughed.

"And you?" he asked me, and I felt ashamed.

"Say, what do you like to take?"

"No, I don't take in the day." I spoke.

"I too don't have time now." Musheer said.

"No formality please." He gave the servant some instruction and said to us, "My eyes were yearning to see you."

"I am really sorry."

"Oh! Yes, the city had spread out. How are you? "

"I am well."

"No."

"Then, Maikada?"

"Please leave it. How long can one continue in business? A man must retire one day.

The servant entered with a tray.

"Pure liquor from France, you met after so long a time. Don't refuse. "

We couldn't reject the offer. It was really an exquisite wine. Ecstasy steadily rose.

He addressed Musheer, "Now tell me how you are doing in America."

"It is not like before. We ran from here because of suffocation, but now it looks like confinement now. We never experienced how difficult it would be to lead a life under the shadow of suspicion. "

"The whole scenario has changed." I said, "The aggressive disobedience against the international verdict on the independence movement and terrorism has been confused. A whole community was frenetically trapped in the net of terrorism. A fire volley is everywhere. A particular community is bearing the brunt. I have no idea who is taking advantage of this situation. No matter who committed the offence, the culprits are ready. The beleaguered culprits are ready. The police also used all the tactics of cruelty. The court never leaves... never leaves. The Dunce community goes deep into the quagmire."

"You become emotional; history changes its colours. Look, Iran sent us out of Iran and

Muslims were rooted out of Spain. We came here after hearing about Asif Jahi's reign. Our ancestors were invited by Salar Jung I. We were made part of the administration. Meer Mahboob Ali Khan bestowed us with rewards. Nawab Sohran Nawaz Jung, Faram Ji Jung, Fareedun-e-Mulk, etc. A Biryani and pearl city, Gujratis and Sindhis also settled here. All had freedom. All of them built their own worship places. They all got aid from government funds. We had a favourable environment here. It was a queer way of living." He said laughingly. "Do you remember? No, you were very young. When we watched a movie, a slide used to appear on the screen where they would perform their obligatory namaz and come back to the theatre. Rind ke rind rahe ,haath se Jannat na gayee, "Paradise did not pass through the hands of libertines."

"Did you like kingship?" I asked.

"No, I like the tolerance of those days." I liked the broad thinking of society. Now the communities have become bigoted. "

"Yes, Muslims also feel great pleasure in using the term. Instead of Khuda Hafiz, Allah Hafiz. I spoke.

"Why did you close Maikada?" Musheer suddenly asked.

"Leave it."

"No, please say, what happened?"

He was quiet for some time, and then said slowly, "Muslims complained that the tavern was very close to a mosque, which was against the law, I was struck with confusion. So, it was a Muslim deed. I thought.

But Maikada and Mosque have been here for a long time.

"It was kingship, now democracy. Since Muslims are the big minority, the government should keep this in consideration."

"Muslims are also becoming hard these days. We started abusing hard Muslims. Musher's intoxication started rising. "

"Why only Muslims?" Sohrab stopped us and said, "We are all growing rigid. Look at me. I didn't get married, because Parsis don't marry outside of their community. Because of this rigid principle, our strength is decreasing. We delay marriages or don't marry. Now there are only 1200 Parsis. "

"Really?"

"The second issue is 'death.'

The same old method: a naked dead body is kept under the hot sun. For nearly two decades, the Vultures avoided the city. People have differences of opinion. Some people say the dead body should be buried. Some people are in favour of cremation. Some favour electric cremation. Some people show an interest in artificially raising vultures. I prefer the ancient method. It is said that if a virtuous man dies, vultures come. I have no idea what will happen to us! According to your belief, the wine traders are internals. He took a deep breath.

"Yes, and also who consumes. God forgives." I spoke.

The servant informed us of dinner. "Why all this formality? We had such nice wine.

Parsi dishes are made for you."

We came to the dining table. I happened to try a Parsi dish for the first time. So, I couldn't refuse the offer.

"This is brown rice. This is Dhanak, lamb, mutton, goat, chicken, or a mixture of lentils like (Arhar, green gram, and urad, eggs, tomatoes, and cucumber.)

What would happen if the vulture didn't come? Would Sohrab's bier burn under the sun? Had Sohrab preferred electric cremation, it would have been better. I was thinking Unintentionally, I looked at the sky. I was remembering the scene from my childhood. A kettle of vultures was coming towards Dakhma.

Parsis' face brightened with joy. After twenty years, the vultures were returning.

"We don't know where they come from," the Parsis asked one another.

"If sugar is dropped on the floor where do ants come from?"

Someone whispered into my ears.

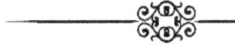

Changing Moments

Bahadur Ali

She passed by me very closely. While passing, a light whiff exploded from her body, and I became crazy after it. My world flourished with the radiance and the fragrance. The impulse had me smitten with her. She was nut-brown, but her features were gorgeous. Had her face not been like Ghazala I wouldn't have been fascinated by her. I was fond of Ghazala. My whole life seemed to be desolated after she left for Pakistan. I have been combating the loneliness ever since she left. When loneliness started stinging, I planned to get married. I bade farewell to my love and began to take an interest in Sameena. She used to frequent the Citizen Club every evening. I had no interest in visiting the club. First of all, I was an ordinary teacher. Second, I didn't like the awful club life. My visit to the club once with Rasheed sparked some interest in me. He was a lawn tennis dabster, and he took an interest in making all his friends lawn tennis players. In this connection, I was introduced to the club as an artist. However, most of the members of the club knew me as an artist, as I practiced art and sold my paintings before taking the job as a teacher. Many members of the club wished me to be a member there, and so I became a member unenthusiastically. Within a short time, my paintings gained fame in society.

Once, the club organized an exhibition of my paintings, and I happened to meet a peart Sameena.

She had a captivating face, and honeyed lips. I was tremendously impressed by her in our first meeting. She was good mannered and an attraction to the club. In the first meeting itself, she parked herself beside me so close that my palms sweated forthwith due to the warmth of fascination. The mist of the gentle aroma of her silky hair stunned me. The scent of her breath enchanted me. I read every desire of hers in my first meeting, which I wanted to. The next moment, she could not make eye contact with me. At the third moment, I got up from there and moved, promising her to meet her the next day. I was feeling as if her grace had captured my mind entirely.

The next day, she arrived as she promised, as I was sure she would do. As the way was convenient, we advanced. She was the only woman in my world.

Hyderabad's mass destruction was caused by police action. In those days, Sameen's father became the victim of police firing as he belonged to 'Razakar Movement.' Her mother got paralyzed much earlier, and she eventually passed away, leaving her alone in the world.

She started staying with one of her uncles. He was a government pleader in a city court. She used to come to the club along with her aunt.

One day, our dream came true. We expressed our desires and tied the knot, becoming one. I forgot the hardships of my past and found joy in her. She was a bright spot in my life. The pleasures doubled as we became one in the spring season.

The next year, Sameena was blessed with a flower child in the same spring season. The next season, one more, and the following year, one more. In three years, we had three kids. However, before the fourth one came, Sameena got offended every now and then. Minor skirmishes began in every matter she felt slighted. I appeased her for hours, but she unwaveringly refused to be convinced. I tried to solve domestic issues at every level, but she couldn't stop being spendthrift.

I know the reason behind her resentment. Those were the days I stopped making my paintings as my eyes became weak due to continual work. My doctor prohibited me from doing this, so my income decreased. I took up teaching, which I left due to a heavy load, and started again and joined a private institution. Now I was making a strategy to lead a teacher's life. Fine, but how could a teacher's wife be a member of a club? How could a specified salaried person of rupees three hundred fifty, afford to buy fashionable, costly dresses? Being exasperated with the burden of three kids and possessing rented utility items at home; I could never dare to bear her expense. I told her, frankly, to cut her coat according to her clothes. She was brought up in a well-to-do family, so she didn't pay heed to it, and rather she took it as criticism.

One day, when she turned up late in the night, I slapped her with obvious discomfort instead of convincing as she was inebriated. She was shocked as I raised my hand for the first time. This incident widened the distances between us. It became her routine; she arrived home late every night, and it used to be a source of contention between us, so we parted ways. I tried every attempt to set her right, but it was inutile. She thought I was an obstacle in her way. I was convinced that she would not come back again, so I divorced her. She gladly accepted the divorce and went to stay with her companion that day. She took nothing from my home except the photos of our children.

Four years passed after Sameena left me. In these four years, many changes occurred: I was promoted as a lecturer, a teacher; my son started speaking like a parrot; Dabbu started living in a hostel; my salary was enhanced, and the cost of living rose. Limits are formed by human, religious, political, social, and linguistic boundaries. Rights altered duties, values, ideologies, and the number of lives. Relationships, love and affection, truth, falsehood, vice and virtue were all thought to be surface level. Every moment changes. In the bounds of these moments, the world changed so much that life again came close to the life of caves and mountains. Thus, everything changed. Sameena changed, I changed, and the whole lot in the world changed. Our paths changed, and we moved on these changed paths like strangers.

Sameena married a club member, a contractor. She was his fourth wife. Sameena's entirely changed beyond recognition. She had forgotten herself. To speak the truth, she had been changing ever since the beginning and she would be changing forever. In these shifting times, who identifies one?

My kith and kin were forcing me to remarry, but I was refusing as I thought of my kids, Pappu and Guddu. The thought of a second mother for my kids makes me shudder. I had witnessed my friend's stepmother's behaviour and her punishment. This thought made me forget the thought of a second marriage. When my kids remember their mother, I used to tell them that she would be back. These days, it is tough for me to convince grown up children.

One day, I went to the airport to go to Bombay to visit Quadri. A few minutes before departure, I **quickened** to take a newspaper. A familiar sound of a call alerted me, "Listen!

I turned and found Sameena standing before me. She approached me. I notice a peculiarity in her. She wasn't the same woman that left me. She was utterly changed. Her white sari-blouse clad moonlight elegance but lacked brightness in her face, and dark circles around her eyes that made me feel that she hadn't slept for many nights. I broke the silence, "What happened to you, Sameena?" Are you okay? "

She was silent for a while and asked, "How are Pappu, Guddu, and Dabbu?"

"They are good; I heard your husband went to America for heart treatment." How is he now? "

"He died."

The contractor's death reminded me of my own. For some time, I simply gazed into the space.

"When did it happen?"

"A few months back."

"Where are you coming from?"

"From Bombay."

"Listen! Our kids always remember you, and I convinced him they would certainly come the next day. I couldn't bring them back to their mother. Do you mind coming with me for a few minutes? "

Sameena couldn't say anything in reply, but her stillness told me the whole thing: she was exhausted from walking on her path.

The Last Stage of The Period of Temptation

Mazharuzzaman Khan

He opened the first door of the book.

He wore an undersized dish-like cap on the back of his head and started grabbing the centuries-old land with both hands that, according to him, the residents of the enlightened and luminous entities kept with them. He was waiting for the wings of an expanse of boundless territory to correspond to the width and length of his reverie. So, when he was grabbing the territory, he looked at the sky over his head and said, "O!" Our beneficent sky, you have stretched the land for us and spread necessities and ingredients for us. Along with them, you have created uncountable animals for us. Oh, sky! It's your benignancy that the white home residents, our frenemies whose God we have crucified, have kept hold of their brains. This is your kindness. Oh, our sky, you have accepted our wishes. This is your kindness. We have entered our commands in the book you sent us. Oh, our sky, our beloved healer is about to arrive as the Euphrates and the Nile are going up and down, they are drying up. We have shaken our hands with the dim-witted community of a region for duping them and perfectly sanitized our hands. We have buried them by drowning them in hot water. O sky, we have laid down our eyes in the reverence of our one-eyed messiah as we hear the bang of his arrival. The final miracle is about to take place. As such, no one can deny that luck favours the audacious.

He opened the book's second door.

All of them were carrying the Ark of the Covenants (Taboot of Sakina) on their heads, and gripping the Babylonians Talmud under their armpits, and standing before the HaiKale Sulaimani, they were reciting, "Hear Shema, O! Israel: the lord our God, the lord is one." They were imitating Akiva by dripping water on their heads, and the heifer was watching them in awe from the top of the mountain. A distant fire was burning, and an innately grim figure was ascending the heights, with the clanging sound of swords heard.5.4 million cadavers whose hands were amputated at the thumbs and genitals were cut by the heart of darkness. Their thumbs were chopped and preserved after severing for counting and recording, because it was evident on their forehead that they were landless people. They don't deserve to occupy a piece of land, or a pond, or a river, so they are always thirsty, and they bleat with thirst.

He opened the book's third door.

It was like a caravan on bare, hot, old land. They kept the pedal to the metal with reverse steps at a loose end, wearing black lace on their eyes and red cotton thrust in their ears. What a nerve! They have dropped ameliorating. You considered self-respect obsolete. You have changed into a malformed person with no spark of decency. Ignoring the writing on the wall, they moved with directionless, reverse steps, raising dust. It looked as if dust was not rising from their movements but was falling or was being poured on their dark bodies. While moving on, one of them said, "I just met a bearded man. He was at his wits' end when he noted no spark of decency in you. He asked me why we were blindfolded and why our ears were stuffed with red cotton. Why are we blindfolded and moving in reverse?

Elvis has left the building, sir. Judge the book by its cover now.

It seems you have lost your reason. You are calling a blind person to the seer and visual. You are asserting an audible to be deaf. You consider our schizophrenia and say that we are walking backwards. However, we are precisely right. We are moving straightforward and the whole world is taking a leaf from our book. Then the bearded man said, "You have thrown caution to the wind." Those who can hear are not hearing and those who can see are not seeing that the seas are quiet now and the drops are roaring. The mountains are hushed, and the grits are boisterous. Nights are awake and days are sleepy. So, lethargy has attacked brains so that dogs are barking, and horses are deep in sleep, so I told the bearded man to leave as he was of no use in this mutinous land as he was barking up the wrong tree. All work ends. Now our purpose remains. So, we are on track to get our purpose solved. We are collecting the mad dogs of every category from every part of the universe to use against the gentle people like you.

Having heard this, the bearded man bent out of shape. Certainly, the blind cannot see...the proud will not. He raised his head and started looking at the sky. You are constantly awake, while everyone else is sleeping. You are constantly awake. One who creates a universe out of grit in the universe, you hear the sound of black ants' chirp in dusk. One who brings life to dead places. One who gives flowers beautiful shapes and a variety of aromas You prepared them as ambrosial. One who gives after death. One who makes streams of milk run from the thin hematic breasts of a man or the udder of an animal. The land you've spread is a shambles. Beasts are roaming everywhere, so amend this belly into the back. The bearded said, "I am feeling sleepy." Then I was also sleepy. I slept while walking. Sleep is the altruistic fortune of the land.

He slowly opened the fourth door of the book and rested his eyes on it. The night was chasing the day, and the day was following the night. Their speed is similar to a horse race. Forty years looks like forty months. In this race, many seasonal scenes and many appealing things from the universe are being flattened. Man is neither sensing that everything is being trampled nor figuring it out. His sensors that trigger a warning have either stopped working or have been disconnected. Whereas fourteen hundred years back you have been fairly and squarely made aware of, nugacity of worldly material and warned against sleep. However, the man is asleep. He is in deep slumber. He is covered with a black bedspread. They were running one after another incessantly. They didn't know that under this boundless roof there was a huge piece of cloth for serving dishes. It was sounded out by people. There were multifarious eateries. All of them fell upon the eateries. They were snatching the eateries from each other. All of them are rapacious. They were gutting. There was no amicability. They are eating face-off. It seems as if they were hungry and thirsty for centuries. Though the table was full of omnifarious foods, they were so caught up in eating that they didn't detect that they had been poured out internally. They were light-planted in their roots crushed under the pile of earthly things. Whereas the voice from the heaven was heard from above to be mindful...Be awake from sleep. You have slept enough. The roof is being dismantled and it is about to topple down. In spite of all the alarms, they couldn't get a grip on themselves. They were asleep. And the roof is about to collapse, and their existence is about to deter them.

He shut the fourth door of the book and opened the fifth door.

When a handful of white people entered the town, they were dazzled. The eyes came out of their sockets. The whole town was living in a dream of ignorance. It looked as if the whole earth were the beds of the town. They were sleeping, unconscious and unaware. Sleep was most likely strewn about. So, a whole handful of people looked towards one another and said, "Perhaps a veil of recklessness was thrown on them or they were beleaguered to sleep."

The previous communities suffered various types of punishment. The punishments have uncountable forms. Gloom descends on a community when it turns its back on reality and enlightenment. So, this town, and many other towns like this, are ill with this. So, slumber is set on them as their comeuppance. And they are lay sleeping. Whenever a community sleeps like this, it is overpowered by some other community. They looked at each other and said, "The men of straw, the vultures of iron holding olives in their beaks, the sun of sand, the reign of crows, blind judges are on the seats of judgment. Nude people, lying on their bellies on the burning sand... glass-made women roaming freely, aimlessly from place to place. According to Mazharuzzaman Khan, its shriveled earth, making its home on water. Scratch your identity with your own hands. They looked at each other, and stated that those who understand gestures, symbols, and indications are no longer trustworthy. They are very rare. Come; let's move from this corner to that corner, as it's getting old to walk from the corner. Those who were cornered are secure now. So, we have to leave this place as soon as possible. When they reached a town, they saw a shining man suddenly assaulted over a despondent body like a leopard and seized the light from his hands and put it in his chest, compressing the dark body and shouting to the people. "O men, have your vision and insight but they both have wounds. Can't you see the bright open light? The enlightened book you have brought to disgrace has become the recipe for disaster. The sacred book you are looking down upon has the obeisance description of your messiah and the holy ayahs describe your savior, which the green-clad recite in their worship and namaz. What a nonsense, undeserved fool you are to dismiss it in a huff without even reading and comprehending its enlightened verses. Indirectly, you discredit your own savior, and stay in white houses with black hearts. Bethink. Paddle your own canoe. Look into it how respectfully your savior is named in it, how graciously his name is mentioned there. You unknowingly you disregard it. Perhaps you have been blinded and made stone deaf.

And he opened the fifth door.

He went near wearer of the scarlet-coloured cloth who was standing on the debris of the building which was dismantled with a bang, "what kind of blast it was? Why this desecration? Why was this house blasted with a bang? They said we were instructed by those who are sitting in the murklins with bleeding hands. Why and what for we don't want to share this secret with you. But before blasting it we have knocked at its door several times, whereas we were not instructed for this. Yet we knocked. Even after knocking the door several times when no one came out. Likewise, we have been instructed to dismantle and destroy many towns. They were vanished in the gloom, and I too had to leave this town as I came here for just one night stay.

He slowly closed the fifth door of the book and opened the sixth one.

There were all types of tall statues found everywhere in a big line in this town. It was in a special uniform under the hot sun. Every person standing in this queue was found with their hands tied at the back. A person with a yellow-coloured chattel was single-mindedly plucking their faces and putting in his chattel. And the lines on their faces were turning to slate, forming a question mark. And those whose faces were removed; these are our faces by birth. Why are you removing them? It made their toes curl. They said, "Our faces are our identities and our early histories. Why are you doing the impossible work of distorting our history and destroying it?" It appears they were restless to feather their nest. They were only told that they had to put on their prepared faces and immerse themselves in their culture. Then, all of a sudden, echoes rise, signaling He closed the sixth door of the book and opened the seventh door and put his eyes on it.

He closed the sixth door and opened seventh door.

Though the minatory situation had existed for some time, the entire town had recently run into the sand, terrified. A mauvais wolf grew into a man eater and he was attacking every town in the night to take away human beings. He gave everyone a hard time. He carried away many human beings day in and day out, so the whole town was horrified. The whole town was down to the wire. Nobody knew which house he would attack, whom he would carry, or how many people would be carried away. So, all the men of the town became alert, or they were sleeping too soundly. They didn't know the history; they neither knew nor perceived such a bad time or knew the weather conditions; they were not up to the speed. But it was too late to realize it. They didn't know how the earth turns from side to side or how the sun fires up. The earth can produce millions of scorpions and snakes. They didn't know anything. The heebie-jeebies situation has been prevailing for years. It attacked one well-known group. He has carried away many human beings. So, the whole town got alarmed. But they didn't want to leave their beds. Sleep attacked their heads. They completely sank into sleep. The wolf attacked all of a sudden. For the first time, they were half asleep and half awake. when frequent attacks proved to be the last straw. They opened their eyes. But it was too late. By this time, many towns had been destroyed. But one fear was still lingering. No one knows what will happen and when? as the small neighboring towns were silent. They were enjoying the situation. They forgot to cry. When a community forgets how to cry, history ignores them. If time and history forget a community, it is understood that their downfall has come. If a community forgets history and time and concentrates on itself, it turns to zero. A zero, which has no value without a number before it or after it. When the wolf destroyed town after town, they looked towards the sky and moved out of their shelter, that night is approaching and the day is coming to an end, wearing a black flag. As a result of his attack, he developed a cataract in his eyes. So, on a dark night, he forgot his way and went astray, reaching a deep cave which was full of lethal animals. So, the cataract made him fall into that cave. He was fated to meet his end like that. When the wolf died in the ditch, everyone in town breathed a sigh of relief and went to their beds, burying themselves in their blankets, as usual. They slept and continued to sleep. Finally, the desert is becoming green and the dead sea, which has the lowest water on earth, is becoming dry and dead as door mail. The Taboote Sakina came out. pandemics raised. The days and nights are cowered(sharank). Iron birds were flying from the threshold of inspiration. But they were asleep. Then suddenly, a clamour erupted and spread all over the earth that the one-eyed had arrived. He had been anticipated for centuries, and now he had arrived. He held the vad of devilish storms in one hand and untold impenetrable obscurities in the other, which he intended to spread throughout the world. When they heard it, they raised their heads from their blankets and slept again. Those who were awake from the early hours were still awake, and a sword was gleaming on the white Minars of Damascus. Its rays were illuminating the entire planet. And then he closed the two flaps of the door, and his eyes came out and fell on the door sill.

In Search of You

Syed Mukarram Niyazi

I have travelled a long distance. I saw so many faces. All of them are my near and dear relatives. Sorry to say I couldn't find the thing I was in search of and continued to search for. I met all the relatives with some or other cover. All people have a cover on their faces. Had their eyes not told the truth, it would have been onerous to find the truth and I would have been deceived...

Eyes cannot be hidden under a veil. They speak what their inner selves say. Just as the eyes are not faithful to the owner, neither is man loyal to anyone in this wide world. Likewise, no one is loyal, neither friends nor relatives. All are selfish. All do trade, giving with one hand and taking with the other. I have been searching for this for years. Since I have grown sensible, I have been busy searching for this. But sorry! I could not get hold of this. Yes, in disguise, hundreds of people deceived me. I have been accepting this deception all knowingly. I think my effort may bloom one day, and I will get it, but how sad it is that it's invincible in my eyes.

I don't know how much time of my life I have spent for the sake of this. I notice A blast from the past. When I look back, I see a long thorny path. The reminiscences of my childhood strike my mind when, once during the autumn, I happen to have a voyage. I stumbled on every step. I had to move cautiously.

Even after covering a long distance, I couldn't catch the shining glow-worm. I don't know how much time of my life I have spent for the sake of this. When I look back, I see a long thorny path. The reminiscences of my childhood strike my mind when, once during the autumn, I happen to have a voyage. I stumbled on every step. I had to move cautiously. Even after covering a long distance, I couldn't catch the shining light worm. I can't seem to get a hold of it. It disappointed me, depriving me of its address. It sparked a passion in me.

As I reach this age, I reflect on my past. When I peep into my past days, I don't know why I visualized the lonely, gloomy night of my past. When I walked cautiously, groping like a blind man, suddenly I drew back in amazement. Whose voice is this in this awesome stillness?

Someone harangued. "Do you think I simply brought you up? No, this is a vain thought. You are highly educated now. Your entry into my business has become non-viable. How long can I carry this weight? To the extent possible, I have given you exemplary training. I have taken care of every requirement. I haven't made you feel inferior anywhere. I did all of this so that you wouldn't be able to deny your responsibilities when the occasion demanded. I am tired now. I must retire. It is time you should occupy my place. "

I wanted to see the face of the speaker, but in this pitch-blackness it was impossible. I go close, near, nearer. The face of this great entity began to appear gradually. Oh no, he's, my father. He loves me very much. I am dearer to him than his life... Then, what's the sense of these sentences? Where's his endearment? No... No, he is not my father. This is not his face. I watched his face closely. I wanted to look for the particular thing in his eyes that I had been searching for. I couldn't find its glimpse. Suddenly, my father's face started blurring. His facial features began to erode. I was stalking him, being surprised. Our shopkeeper's face took its place. The shopkeeper, whom I frequented from my childhood for groceries, and he exchanged items for money. He used to take money with one hand and hand over the groceries with the other.

I was on the horns of a dilemma. Was the expression of love and affection dealt with? Was it an imposture? Was it a ruse that I had been subjected to since childhood? I didn't have the nerve to accept this spice... I got overturned in a shocked and petrified state. Unpalatable Suddenly, I began running from there. Despite leaving the place, I could not get rid of the familiar voice that was chasing me. It is still echoing in my ears from far behind.

I always bore with the difficulties and nurtured you tenderly and gave you a sniffing future. Buoyed you to live in society with a raised head... Now you must be in my service. I am running. I had been running continuously when I stumbled in the darkness and was about to fall to the earth when two hands supported me. Who are you? I questioned being afraid. I am... Don't you regret saying this? Do you know who I am? What an era! Oh my God! I didn't know you would pay no attention to me or ignore my obligations so soon. I have been with you since childhood. I have held you up in every frail situation. Whenever you required support, I have lent you a hand. You have ignored me suddenly. Is it your friendship? You forgot your childhood friend. Is it your right behavior? I tried to identify him sheepishly.

The darkness slowly cleansed his face. Oh! This is my childhood intimate friend. But what about these words, these sentences, and his remonstration? I tried to probe the something in his eyes which I had been looking for, but no, there was not even a shade of it...I found there only the necessities and selfish motives. His face started to vary slowly. I sprang up as I faced disappointment again. I started running again. The echoes continued to come from behind. "Hear... here for a while... I'm feeling tense these days. My company completely failed... debtors are worrying me. I am surviving in anticipation of your fiscal support. I cry for your mercy. I was running, being flabbergasted. I found darkness all around me, and the way is long. I stopped for a while to relax. I was panting for breath. At that moment, I sensed the soft touch of a delicate hand, and a mellifluous voice touched my ears.

Where are you running like this? What's your worry now? Think of me too. I can no longer put a cripple in front of my father. By the grace of God, you have expanded a booming business. What's the delay now? For your sake, I have rejected many good matches. It's your responsibility now to send a marriage proposal to my house. How long can I wait like this?

I am startled. This feminine tone has a complaint full of love. I tried to identify it. Yes, she is my first and final love. I passionately loved this innocent maiden of purity with intact sincerity, whereas her sentences embarrassed me. Despite all this, I looked into her eyes as I was sure that I would find the thing I was looking for.

I am shocked. No, I didn't find the thing I was searching for. The face with blue eyes is also transforming step by step. Her face has changed into the face of the bank's lady cashier's face, from which I can draw my deposited amount only after presenting a check. Is this an analogous matter here? Give and take. I was puzzled, so I started running. The feminine echo was following me. "No, don't leave me alone at this juncture. I have sacrificed many things for your sake. Please? Don't be this ruthless...

Once again, I started running on this long, serene road. The feelings of tiredness have taken me into custody. I want to stop for a while and relax, but I fear that I might become an altar to some selfish faces. While running, I collided with a person who was coming from the opposite side and staggered.

"Are you blind? " I asked, in irritation.

"Excuse me, brother."

This sound... this sound... I started examining this sound.

It looks like an old sound. I go close to him to pry further. Yes, this is my bruh, Amman-jaya, my younger brother. I recalled something specific and fixed my eyes on his face. He himself was not speaking, but his eyes were speaking a lot.

"I was always your well-wisher, bother. I prayed for your success and bright futures in the night. I have supported you in every field during your academic career. I shouldered the responsibility of bringing groceries.

As I always had your academic career in my mind, I tried to keep you away from all sorts of domestic tribulations. Now you are capable of supporting others. Yes, brother, I want to go to the Middle East to better my future, and I have the qualifications, eligibility, and skills to do so. Please give me the Dubai visa, brother."

I was unnerved. The castle of my hopes was razed as the image of the shopkeeper appeared on the face of my brother. He had some sure speculation that his investments wouldn't go haywire and that he would get good returns from his investments, quid-pro-quo, 'give with one hand and take with the other.'

I overlooked his eyes and took my way forward, utterly exhausted. I was hot under the collar as I travelled a long distance. I met many familiar faces. All of them were of my kith and kin, but it's a pity that I couldn't get the distinct thing I was searching for and will be searching for.

All faces are encased. All people have a cover on their faces. It's written all over their face. Had their eyes not told the truth, it would have been onerous to find the truth and, I would have been deceived... Eyes cannot be hidden under a veil. They speak what their inner selves say. Just as the eyes are not faithful to the owner, neither is man loyal to anyone in this wide world. Likewise, no one is loyal, neither friends nor relatives. All are selfish. All do trade, giving with one hand and taking with the other. We all struck a bargain.

I am going forward on this dark, howling path. Many episodes have taken place on the way. Nevertheless, I continued my search. I will not be in peace until I find it. My mind is overcast with clouds unless I find the specific thing. I cannot get liberation.

"Excuse me please!" Someone addressed me from somewhere in the darkness. I have my cousin's wedding next week. This time I want a silver embroidered sari. You evaded my request to buy me a sari for my maternal cousin's marriage. But you have to fulfill my desire this time. How long will you keep me diverted like this? I have taken dissidence of my parental home by marrying you. For your sake, I have rejected many standard proposals for three years, and you still can't afford to buy me a sari. On the other hand, you hand over a large amount to your parents. You arrange for yourself to send your younger brother to Dubai. You help your selfish friends every now and then, and you think it is your responsibility to bear all the expenses of your sister's marriage, but for me, your love and this thrift. "

I could notice the hidden hint of cynicism in these cherished words of my wife. I want to see clearly the unique thing in her eyes, which I discovered immediately after our marriage. But now even its glimpse is untraceable. My wife's face is also transforming little by little.

My wife's sarcastic tone has reminded me of my mother and the moment of wilderness that I once came across. I had full confidence that my quest would be completed in my mother's eyes. I put up with the burden of your creation in my womb for nine months; breastfed you for two years and tolerated many adversities to make a human being. Do you want to marry a female of your choice in exchange? Don't I have the right to select one for you? Have I raised you to select a better half for yourself? Your highly educated cousin has agreed to marry your sister on the condition that you marry his well-behaved and comely sister. "Can't you accept this proposal for your sister's welfare in exchange for my sacrifices?" I was feeling blue. Thus, my mother also considers me an ordinary chess pawn to swindle and beat the opponents' chessman. Are my emotions not emotions? Don't I have a sense of self? With disenchantment, I make an attempt to see the answers to my questions in my mother's eyes. Which I had been running in the dark night. My mother also wholly lacks that. I could hardly tolerate that jerk. I found in my sister's eyes the question of dowry. I had to pay her as a tribute of thanks in exchange for that. And now...

Now I am fully tired from running on this long and dark night. My nerves have become infirm. though I still have a long way to go. but it seems my search is to no avail. I thought it might be the rarest, if not extinct. But in this mechanical and 'give and take' world, it is no more.

So, I dropped the observation of faces. I don't have the guts to do it anymore, as I am afraid of being deceived.

Now I want to end this journey on this muted note soon, so that I may go to the other end, where light is waiting for me, where I can liberate myself from this unfathomable gloom. So, I made my pace fast. I am running...Fast, faster, the fastest.

Despite my attempts to be speedier, there came an irrepressible difference in my speed all of a sudden. Unwillingly, I had to stop because someone called me from darkness after a long gap, in a weak voice, very low note.

"Pa, Pa, Papa..."

I rushed towards the sound.

"Papa... papa...Where are you?" are you going, leaving me here? I will join you, papa. "

I sat on my knees and pulled the kid towards me. Oh! It is my son.

"Certainly, my son... certainly." I wanted to take him in my arms, but my anxious eyes contacted his in his eyes, having no control as I am used to do'

1. I sprang up from my place not due to wonder but due to tremendous mirth.

After an ardent long search, I eventually got it in my son's shining eyes, pure, candid, and altruistic.

What should I name my eyes? The reflection of which I am seeing in my son's eyes, and the image of my eyes that longs to extort for my blessing training that I bestowed upon him

www.ingramcontent.com/pod-product-compliance
Lightning Source LLC
LaVergne TN
LVHW061615070526
838199LV00078B/7286